THE SILK ROUTE SPY

ENAKSHI SENGUPTA

THE SILK ROUTE SPY

THE TRUE STORY OF AN INDIAN DOUBLE AGENT

HARPER
NON-FICTION

First published in India by Harper Non-Fiction 2024
An imprint of HarperCollins *Publishers*
4th Floor, Tower A, Building No. 10, DLF Cyber City,
DLF Phase II, Gurugram, Haryana – 122002
www.harpercollins.co.in

2 4 6 8 10 9 7 5 3 1

Copyright © Dr Enakshi Sengupta 2024

P-ISBN: 978-93-6213-011-2
E-ISBN: 978-93-6213-570-4

The views and opinions expressed in this book are the author's
own and the facts are as reported by her, and the publishers
are not in any way liable for the same.

The book is based on real events, recreated through first-hand accounts
and/or narrated anecdotes. In instances, names have been changed, events
compressed and dialogues have been recreated.

Dr Enakshi Sengupta asserts the moral right
to be identified as the author of this work.

All rights reserved. No part of this publication may be reproduced,
stored in a retrieval system, or transmitted, in any form or by any
means, electronic, mechanical, photocopying, recording or otherwise,
without the prior permission of the publishers.

Typeset in 11.5/15.2 Adobe Garamond at
HarperCollins *Publishers* India

Printed and bound at
Replika Press Pvt. Ltd.

This book is produced from independently certified FSC® paper to ensure
responsible forest management.

'I am because you are.'
This book is dedicated to my late husband, Vijay Kapur,
who continues to remain my inspiration

PROLOGUE

Every child has a hero, someone they would like to emulate. My husband Vijay Kapur's hero was his grandfather, Nandlal Kapur. When Vijay came to this planet, he heard that his grandfather rushed from Punjab and went straight to Newmarket to buy a huge, red-coloured pram for the large baby. Vijay's earliest memories were of sitting beside his grandfather and listening to the tales of a faraway land, heroic stories of survival and patriotism. Those tales often transported him to a land of imagination, across a dark turbulent sea, where a red lantern hung on the doorstep and a bowl of rice porridge was eaten on a full moon day. Sometimes he would try to wear the heavy war helmet, olive in colour but which had begun rusting along the edges while it was stashed under the bed. At times he would cry to accompany his grandfather to Fort William (army base) and would not understand why his grandmother looked different from others and why his grandfather wore long shirts with buttoned straps on his shoulder, unlike any other old man in the vicinity.

At times he questioned, but most of the time he didn't ask them fearing that it would irritate his ageing grandfather and he would not get the coin from him that would fetch a roasted corn cob or an orange ice cream lolly.

Long after his grandfather's demise, sitting on a couch in the famous 'Malaya peninsula' (Kuala Lumpur), Vijay would narrate those tales to his wife (me). Watching a Shaolin movie together he would say, 'This must be what Shanghai looked like at that time when my grandfather was there. See the red cheongsam, those red lanterns and the impeccably dressed gentry.'

The story took shape in bits and pieces in my mind, and I would often imagine a young man from Punjab navigating those lanes. My imagination was triggered whenever Vijay talked about his grandfather. 'You know he was a British spy. Everyone knew him as a silk trader. That was his identity in Japan, where he met and married my grandmother. In reality, he was a spy who also helped and contributed to the independence movement.'

I would hanker to hear more. 'That's very interesting, tell me more about him. Where was your village? How did he get into it …' and the conversation would last till the wee hours of the morning. Occasionally, Vijay would get up and stand in front of the window and look at the glittering Petronas Twin Towers in the distance. Then he would turn around and remark, 'Strange, that I, too, ended up coming to the far east, here, to the Malaya peninsula, so close to Johor Baru where our family took shelter during the war.'

Then one day Vijay too left this world, just twenty-one days after his fiftieth birthday. I was left with memories and lots of photographs. Rummaging through them on a nothing-much-to-do day, I kept staring at a particular photo from

PROLOGUE

1932 taken in a studio in Japan. It was of Vijay's grandfather, smartly dressed, holding his firstborn in his lap. Then more photos of his Japanese wife (my grandmother-in-law), their children, and of course the picture of the pram with little Vijay sleeping in it. The more I discovered, the more I felt this immense urge to tell the story of Nandlal, a young boy from Punjab who travelled the world.

Despite my apprehension about tackling this deeply personal yet complicated story from the past, I started writing. I kept thinking about how to glue the bits and pieces that I had heard from Vijay together. Nandlal Kapur was a widely travelled man who traversed countries, which was not very common in those days. I wanted to follow a chronological sequence, but certain parts of his life were shrouded in a mist. I decided to start talking about young Nandlal and his much-loved Firozpur. I traced what I heard, and I reconstructed some of the finer details. I went with Nandlal from Firozpur to Amritsar and then to the rest of India. I sailed with him, huddling with him on the lower deck of a ship, imagining how claustrophobic it must have been for him. My heart palpitated when he escaped from Shanghai and worried when he burned with fever in Rangoon. The picture of my father-in-law looking princely in his attire in Japan filled me with pride. I felt delighted to be able to live all those moments with him.

How often do we believe in the supernatural? Our mind tries to rationalize what is unexplained. Yet, here I believe that Nandlal Kapur wanted me to tell his story and he guided me from chapter to chapter, from one destination to the next, narrating his trials and tribulations.

Sometimes I sit back and wonder if I have been able to do justice to his work and his memories. I have tried my best to collect the scattered pearls of his life story and string them together for everyone to see and admire the work of an unknown son of the motherland.

FIROZPUR

1

From a distance, one could spot Prito Devi hunched on a small stool, her body moving slowly in a rhythmic sway. A thick mist hung from the trees. Prito looked up. There was something ominous in the air, an impending gloom. It was as if deep sadness lurked in the leaves, mixed with grime, dust and fog. She shook her head. Her mother-in-law, God have mercy on the kind soul, had always told her to avoid negative thoughts as they heralded unpleasant events. She coaxed herself to return to reality as she had much to do. A brass vessel filled with ripe and plump yellow lemons from her tree stood before her. She planned to wash them and then rub them on the grinding stone to smoothen their skins before bottling them as a pickle.

Suddenly, Prito looked up. She could hear a metallic clack. Her firstborn, Nandlal Kapur, her beloved Nandu, was bent over his bicycle, trying to fix the chain. Nandu had taken after his father—tall and broad-shouldered with a long, sharp nose and thick hair that was combed back. His complexion was very fair, like his mother's. In the winter, his cheeks took on a pinkish hue. He sat on his haunches, his kurta stretched over his wide shoulders, sleeves rolled back over strong arms, ferociously fixing the chain. Nandu turned back and smiled at his mother. Prito always thought that her son had lovely large eyes that were filled with kindness, yet they also seemed to carry a forlorn look as if staring at something in the distance. A thought crossed her mind. She had to get her son married soon. Perhaps then the forlorn look would go away. She decided to talk to her husband. Anyone would be happy to give their daughter's hand in marriage to Nandu.

Nandu, realizing that his mother had been staring at him for a while, got up, wiped his hand on a wet cloth, and came to sit beside her. 'You are always lost in thought when you make pickles. Thinking about my marriage, I guess? Probably imagining the sweets you will make, or wondering whether to call a halwai?' he chuckled.

Prito shook her head. 'Don't make fun of your old mother. I am always thinking about your well-being. Where do you go in the afternoons? You still don't have a job. I was told that you go to the sahib's kothi a lot. You know, the atmosphere in the country is not good; people are against these angrez, the British. I have heard that there have been a lot of killings and protests. Don't get mixed up in politics. Na! It is not good for you or us. You have two younger brothers to think of as well. You must try and get a good job soon.'

Nandu put an arm around his mother. 'That is what I am doing, Bebe, that is what I am doing. I am trying to get a job at the post office. You know how important a post office is. It will be the job of a lifetime.'

Prito nodded.

Nandu continued. 'Such jobs don't come easy. These days there are many boys who have completed their matriculation.

From our college alone there are more than twenty. You think I stand a fair chance?'

Prito pushed the brass vessel closer to where Nandu was sitting. Her voice was shrill, which usually happened when she defended her case. 'Why not? You look good, you are smart, and you speak proper English. Soon, you will have a sarkari job.' She mellowed down, but continued muttering to herself, 'I must start preparing for your wedding. Remember to take me to the bazaar. I need to begin by buying a few yards of silk for your outfit.'

Nandu touched his mother's shoulder and tried to distract her from the topic at hand. But then he sighed. He knew there was no point arguing with either of his parents. They were both stubborn and would ultimately do what they wanted to. He needed to work fast if he intended to realize his dreams. Once he had a wife, it would be difficult. He would be holding crying babies instead of nursing his dreams. He knew he was in a difficult situation and felt guilty knowing that he would have to lie to his mother.

Last week, he had been recruited as an informer for the British regiment stationed at his village. He was not at liberty to talk about it, so he pretended that he was scouting for a job. The thrill and the adrenaline rush that he had experienced at being offered his first job had diminished when he realized it had to be kept a secret.

Unmindfully, he stuck a finger into the mound of spices and tasted it. It was a concoction of rock salt, chilli powder, dried mango and tamarind powder, a special recipe handed down to his mother from his grandmother.

His mother noticed and slapped him hard on the wrist. 'Don't put your saliva in the spices. The pickle will rot. How many times have I told you this? Put out your palm. I will give you a spoonful to lick.'

Nandu got up, brushed the dirt off his kurta, and said, 'Bebe, I need to go and meet some friends. They are waiting for me at the chowk. I will savour the spices when the pickle is ready.'

Prito knew that something was bothering her son. She tried to ease the situation by saying, 'Next Sunday, you must visit your sister. You know how much she adores you. I have made some sweets using white sesame seeds. It will be good for her at this time and will help her body make more blood. You must also get me some tender mustard leaves from the field. I will make sarson da saag just the way she likes it, with extra garlic and chilli. I have heard that her mother-in-law cannot make it the way I do!'

Nandu, who had begun pedalling his cycle, looked back and said, 'Sure, I will do that!'

As Nandu cycled out of the gate, Prito's younger son, Dhyanchand, entered. She called out to him, 'Dhannu, where have you been? You look muddy. Just look at the back of your shirt. Were you with Rani's daughter again in the mustard field, or was it sugarcane this time? If you get caught once more, your father will peel the skin off your back. You rogue, why can't you be more like your elder brother? You behave like a landlord's son, whose only interest is running around in the fields and chasing young girls. One more complaint and you are dead, my son. Don't come crying to me, asking me to save you from your father's wrath. This time, I won't.'

Dhyanchand laughed as he washed his feet using water from an iron bucket kept nearby. 'Bebe, I am not my brother. We are not alike, and you know that. Wait till I get you a doll-like bride. Your anger will melt. Now give me some roti with a piece of radish and chilli. I am famished.'

The sun smiled at the banter and decided to set for the day. The birds, too, settled down in the mango tree. The aroma from the lemons and spices filled the thick, misty wind that came with the approaching dusk. It seemed like the most peaceful and happy corner in the world.

2

Nandu knew he was late. Cycling as fast as he could past the red-brick quarters of the British officers, he marvelled at the history and heritage of Firozpur. It was around the late 1800s that the British had decided to grow their presence here, and Firozpur had become the 'eyes of the British Raj'. Their aim was to gather information about the Lahore Darbar and to monitor the activities of the Sikh community who were grouped under Maharaja Ranjit Singh as the Sikh court.

Everywhere around Firozpur, one could see the signs of prosperity. Large bungalows that housed British officials and their families, big official buildings, roads, railways, bridges, sprawling lawns and shops adorned the town. *Is this prosperity something one has to thank the ruling Raj for and a reason to keep serving them? Or is it becoming the cause of the resentment that is slowly spiralling and engulfing the country like thick smoke?* The thought left Nandu perplexed. Knox Road, only five miles away from the Sutlej river, looked beautiful in the early winter with its brick houses and flowers. Nandu's chest swelled with pride at belonging to such an important and strategic place. The Firozpur cantonment did not have fertile agricultural land like the rest of Punjab, but its connectivity through railroad had prompted trade to flourish. Nandu's father worked in the Sutlej Flour Mill, the largest in Punjab and probably the entire country. He felt proud as he meandered his way through the shops that sold the finest products from across the world. *Someday, I, too, will own a big shop.*

Nandu realized that he had slowed down on account of his daydreaming. It was not the time to admire Firozpur. He doubled his speed, pedalling as fast as possible. The new officer in charge, Charles*, to whom he had to report, was not fond of waiting.

A new and impatient young member of the cantonment, Charles had arrived from the Lucknow Residency recently. Nandu had tried to befriend him several times, but the officer didn't seem to believe in making friends with the 'natives'. Attempts to share a cigarette, or his mother's handmade laddoos, had fallen flat. Charles's job was to train Nandu, and he preferred to stick to that.

Nandu somehow secured his cycle to a tree nearby. The gravelly road leading up to the cantonment building was nearly a five-minute walk. His thin slippers didn't make the brisk walk easy as the gravel pricked at the soles. Nevertheless, he made quite an effort to race up the fifty steps to Charles's office. By the end, he could hear shallow breaths hissing out of his lungs.

Before entering the office, Nandu wiped the sweat away with his sleeves. He made a mental note to exercise more and cut down on the ghee that his mother heaped on his rotis.

---

* *Name changed*

After all, he was barely in his twenties, and the path that he had chosen demanded physical fitness.

Charles was not happy. In his thick British accent, he emphasized the word 'Lal'. 'Nand*lal*, you are late again! Do you realize that a few seconds may one day cost you your life? This is not a joke, my dear boy. This is not a joke. You can still withdraw your name if you wish to.'

Nandu replied meekly. 'I am sorry, sir. It will not happen again. You will find that I am your best choice, sir.'

The young officer, softening at being addressed as 'sir', said, 'And where are you with your training and learning about the trade? You need to know it like the back of your hand!' He turned his hand to show the back of his palm, revealing its rising blue veins.

'I am reading the book you gave me. I am learning all about cocoons, larvae, spinning, etc. But, sir, I have a problem with the machine. I can't practise at home. I don't have a separate room; I sleep with my brothers. In our culture, we don't close doors unless we are married and sleeping with our wife,' Nandu said, blushing a bit.

Charles chuckled. 'Get married then. Put your wife to sleep and practise. You need to master the code fast. My dear boy, one can never learn a trade by reading books about cocoons. You are supposed to sit in Lalaji's shop and help him with the sales. He is our man. He will help you with what you need to know to master the trade. It has already been arranged. Why the delay?'

Nandu distractedly started picking at a chip of wood from the table with his long fingers.

Charles noticed. 'Do you want to ask me something? Tell me, I am all ears.'

Nandu cleared his throat. 'Sir, I can sit in Lalaji's shop every day till the evening and then come here to practise the code, but if I am gone the whole day and do not work on the farmland, my parents expect me to earn money. I don't get paid here, and I am not sure whether Lalaji will give me anything. This Sunday, I am supposed to visit my married sister, sir. I don't even have enough money to take a gift. I want to give her a dozen shiny glass bangles that she likes, or a parandi, the ribbons made with silk thread. It is embarrassing for me to keep asking my father for pocket money. After all, I am a grown man and the eldest son.'

Charles shifted in his chair, took out two rupee notes from his wallet, and gave them to Nandu. 'Go buy those bangles for your sister. Ah! Sisters! They can be real pests. You love to hate them and hate to love them. I have a couple of them, too. When I go home, all they are interested in is plundering my box for their share of the goodies. Sometimes they even forget to greet me!' he said with an amused smile.

Seeing Charles share a personal moment, Nandu mustered up the courage and asked, 'Sir, may I ask you for a favour?'

'What now, Nandlal? You natives always seem to ask for favours. Go ahead, spit it out, my boy. I don't have the whole evening to listen to you. There is a party at the cantonment.'

Nandu hated being called a 'native', but he controlled his resentment. 'Sir, may I come here on Sunday evening and practise the code? I am supposed to visit my sister, but I can pretend that I was kept back at her place.'

'All right, all right. You may come on Sunday. I will tell the orderly to open the office room for you. Also, Lalaji will give you two rupees per week. I will try to arrange something, too, so that you can earn a handsome amount. Now run along and don't waste my time, boy. Things are not getting easier for us in your country. Lots to handle. Lots to handle and manage.'

Nandu quietly left the room. He felt good about the money. Papaji would be happy.

Nandu didn't have an office, so to say, in the cantonment. Instead, he had a table and a chair where old files, newspapers, and broken furniture were stored amidst dust and cobwebs. He sneezed every time he entered the damp and dusty room. That Sunday, on a broken chair, he spotted an old newspaper. The headline declared that Lala Lajpat Rai had succumbed to a head injury. He and others had been protesting against the Simon Commission when they were mercilessly beaten up by the British. Something twisted inside Nandu's chest. He nearly threw up, just about managing to gulp the bitter bile that rose in his mouth. Anger and resentment leapt up in his heart. 'They treat us like dogs. We are not even allowed to protest in our own country,' he murmured to himself. His jaw hardened as he said, 'Someday, someday soon …' His voice trailed off; he was not quite sure what he could do. He clenched his fist and sat down to master Morse code.

Nandu felt a twinge of guilt brewing inside him. He was working for the British when people his age were fighting for the country's freedom and embracing death. Brushing aside all thoughts of what could be and what was, he concentrated on the dashes and the dots, and then moved his hand rhythmically on a lever attached to the wooden machine. His ears were filled with the beeps, both the small and long ones. He listened hard to identify the five distinct sounds and increased his speed. He had to memorize the alphabet before cycling home. *Focus, Nandu, focus!*

Back home, dinner was a ritual that no one could escape. Papaji would sit down, evoke the name of the deity and say thanks for the meal. Next to him would sit his eldest son and then the two younger boys. Their mother, Prito, would stand beside the kitchen door, watchful of everyone's plate, stepping in to fill up the bowls with dal, or put a hot roti or two on the plates while instructing the housemaid to hurry up.

Occasionally, she would step in to put on their plates some pickle or sweet that she had made in the afternoon. She would always pull her dupatta over her head and walk noiselessly.

Dinner was also the time when Papaji would discuss important issues pertaining to the family, the village, the farmland and, occasionally, politics. Mostly though, he avoided the topic. He was cautious about his sons not getting caught up in politics. The last thing he wanted was to see them jailed or losing their lives in a shootout or lathi-charge.

That night, Nandu carefully broke his roti with two fingers, cleared his throat and addressed his father. 'Papaji, I think I have got a job.'

'Yes? Go on,' said Papaji. 'Where?'

'Nearby. In Lalaji's shop. A friend of mine arranged it. I will have to be there till the afternoon. After that, I will go to the cantonment to write some letters, sort the post, maybe take dictation from a junior officer. Lalaji will pay me two rupees per week. I will also get some money from the cantonment. I am not sure how much, but I am hoping it will be eight to ten rupees.'

Papaji chewed contemplatively on a piece of roti. 'Good, very good. That means around twenty rupees per month. I was not sure if you would like to sit in a shop and sell clothes. But if that is what you want, go ahead.'

'I am not fond of selling, but I want to learn the trade so that I can have a shop of my own someday. Maybe I can employ people, too. Plus, the money isn't bad. We can start some repair work in the house with the extra cash. This season, the crops were not good either. And I don't know how long the local mill will buy our mustard to press oil. The economy of our country is on shaky ground.'

Papaji looked at his wife. 'Prito, our son has grown up. He talks about responsibilities and the economy. I think we have brought him up well!' he said with a smile and picked up the tumbler of buttermilk.

The youngest born, Balraj, who was usually quiet, mustered up the courage and addressed his eldest brother.

'Paaji, when you get your salary, will you buy me a cricket bat? I don't like borrowing one from Jagjit. He gives it to me, but then he acts as if he is doing me a favour.'

Nandu laughed out loud. 'Sure, I will. But both you and Dhyanchand need to go to the field and oversee the labourers from now on as I might not have much time. Bebe, I want you to please pack some lunch for me. Two rotis and a bit of pickle will do. You will pack a small box, won't you?'

Prito Devi smiled. 'Your lunch box might also have halwa on some days.'

'I want halwa, too!' Balraj chimed in.

Everyone laughed. Ballu, as Balraj was fondly called, loved his food. The dollops of fat hanging on him were evidence enough. The youngest in the family, he was thoroughly pampered by everyone.

Later that night, Nandu decided to sleep in the open and not in the crowded room with his brothers. He wanted to think. Some careful planning needed to be done. As he pulled his razai around him, he heaved a sigh of relief. So far, everything was going as planned. Everyone was happy, and nothing gave him more contentment than seeing his family smiling and enjoying a meal together.

Nandu started calculating how he would divide his day. He needed to visit the farmland, too. He could not simply dump the responsibility on his younger brothers, especially since he knew that his father wouldn't have the time either. He also counted how many months he had to learn the trade of silk clothes, coupled with his reading and the time he needed to master other skills. As an informer, he would have to learn how to shoot as well. The thought of holding a pistol made him nervous, yet it gave him an adrenaline rush. He only hoped that he would pass all the tests smoothly. Then, a life full of adventures would open before him, a life that he had always dreamt of.

The trees in the courtyard swayed with the wind. The rustling of the leaves lulled Nandu into deep sleep.

3

A month passed. Nandu was fully immersed in his training. Every morning, he cycled out to Lalaji's shop. Since Lalaji was paying him two rupees a week, he expected Nandu to open the shop, dust the corners, fill the jug and even bring him tea from a nearby shop. Generally considered a fatherly figure, Lalaji was quite friendly and helpful when it came to his employees, but his expectations at times breached the usual boundary between an employer and an employee, especially when it came to running errands.

Nandu did not mind. Lalaji was almost his father's age, and his expanding girth and gout didn't help his mobility. Nandu thought there was no harm in fetching a cup of tea or filling up the water jug. Most of the time, Lalaji could not reach the upper shelves and Nandu was called to help bring the merchandise down. Each time, Lalaji cracked the usual joke. 'When are we going to take advantage of your height, son, if not now?'

Nandu, meanwhile, tried to grasp all he could about silk. Charles was right. The book could not teach him much beyond cocoons and larvae. There was so much to learn about this natural textile that had originated in China, be it the six hundred thread count or the sheen.

Japanese silk was flooding the market. Kinsha and Omeshi were considered the best varieties because they reflected light. As a result, they were priced much higher than the other varieties.

Sometimes, Nandu accompanied Lalaji to Zohra Man Singh's* residence, an influential leader and businessman in the region. Singh had several daughters and daughters-in-law whose only job seemed to be getting new clothes stitched. They never visited the shops though. Nandu carried the bundle of fresh imports while Lalaji used his gift of the gab to convince the women to buy the new lot. Nandu often observed the women eyeing him, but he preferred to keep to himself. He was on a mission and could not afford to lose focus. Every day, he waited for dusk, when he would run to the cantonment and practise Morse code. He needed to master it by the end of the month.

Apart from Morse code, Nandu was being trained rigorously to maintain his fitness. He was made to cross man-made hurdles, do high and long jumps, swim and run for miles. He would often go home dog-tired, making his mother wonder what left her son so exhausted. She was surprised that merely sitting in a shop and selling clothes could tire her young son out like that.

Next on Nandu's list was practising interrogations. For this, he would be cornered by Charles, who would then grill and cross-question him to extract information. At times, Nandu was asked to interrogate a junior officer, just to sharpen his skills. He was also trained in physiology and taught the pressure points and vulnerable spots in the human body that could kill or maim a person. He was also given a book about poisoning, from which he acquired theoretical knowledge. However, he already knew the antidotes for a few commonly available poisons and their effects on the body.

It took him a couple of months to master these skills, including using a knife to kill or gravely injure a person. He looked forward to being trained to use a gun.

Sundays were reserved for Nandu's best friend, Ajit Pal Singh. Ajit had been his friend, confidant and partner in crime since school. Unfailingly on each Sunday, after lunch, Nandu went to meet Ajit behind the gurdwara. They smoked a cigarette or two, sometimes got hot samosas and sweetened milk tea from Kanhaiya Lal's sweet shop and poured their hearts out to each other.

For some time, Ajit had been feeling low. 'Yaara, it is almost time for you to leave. A few more months, isn't it? What will I do once you go? Who will sit with me and chat and bite into these samosas? More importantly, who will pay for them?'

Nandu playfully poked Ajit in the ribs. 'We will be friends forever. I don't even remember when we became friends. It was before we started going to school, I think. Remember, when we were teenagers, how we used to climb the tamarind tree after school to see big-breasted Asha?' He chuckled at the memory. 'We nearly got caught as a bee entered your gaping mouth. She got married. I wonder where she is now. Do you remember how we used to go to that shop in Mirza Wali Gali to have kebabs and biryani and could never pay for them? We aimed to run most of the time, but Mirza Chacha was kind. He didn't mind feeding two hungry lads.'

Ajit sighed. 'Yes, those were the good old days. We were not in a hurry to grow up, we didn't have a career to choose or a dream to follow. Kebabs and samosas were our only dreams apart from Asha,' he said and started laughing. Then, suddenly, he went very quiet and turned towards his friend. 'Nandu, may I ask you something?'

'Sure,' said Nandu.

'Are you sure, yaara, that this is what you want? That this is your dream? Away from your family, away from your world, in an obscure faraway country where people don't talk like you, dress like you, or eat like you? And that job? You might not come back home; you might be buried in a strange country. What if your parents come to know? They will be marked as a traitor's family, especially when the atmosphere in the country is so charged. Is this what you want, my friend?'

Nandu lowered his voice. 'I am sure that this is the only way I can fulfil my dreams. We were not born into rich families, otherwise it would have been natural for us to sail to Oxford or Cambridge, waving our silk handkerchiefs at our families. What else can I do? I cannot imagine a life in this village, picking mustard leaves, marrying a Lakshmi or a Lajwanti, and teaching my kids to cycle over the muddy roads. There is no future here. I wanted you to enrol in the programme, too, but you are stubborn. You are happy tending to your farmland and looking after your cattle. I am never going to tell my parents. As far as they are concerned, I will be doing a regular job in another city, or perhaps another country. Besides, I want to be a part of the system and destroy it from within, like a termite. I know my secrets are safe with you. If you betray me, I shall spill the beans about Asha,' he said, shaking his head and laughing.

Ajit looked grim. 'Be careful, my friend. You are walking on a dangerous road. I don't know what goes on inside that head of yours. Nobody does. Everyone wants to become a tiger or a lion, but my friend here wants to be a termite. People use poison to kill termites, just remember that,' he said, patting Nandu on the head.

As the sun set, the two friends parted ways, hugging each other with a twinge of sadness and the melancholic gloom of impending separation.

The month, which had started on a monotonous tone with Nandu filling up Lalaji's water jug, didn't end so badly. Nandu kept busy with an increasing amount of work as part of his training. He clearly remembered that evening when, right before dinner, he had pushed his first salary of twelve rupees into Papaji's palm and given the small gifts he had purchased for everyone in the family. His father had hugged him tight and kept patting his back. He seemed to have lost his voice. Nandu could see his eyes glistening. His mother had made kheer and ensured that she added extra ghee to Nandu's parathas. Balraj had been excited about his bat and had kept posing with it, raising it and striking an imaginary ball. Happiness and warmth had overflowed in the Kapur household.

Nandu, however, felt torn. He wondered if he should continue living a life full of warmth, familial love and laughter, or tread down an uncharted path. Both roads seemed alluring to him. His thoughts led to a disturbed night, causing him to toss and turn on his charpoy under the open sky.

Four months had passed in the training and then came the day when Charles handed over a Webley revolver to him. 'This beauty is yours from today. Take good care of it,' he said.

Nandu had never been so scared. His hands shook and he felt shivers run down his spine. He broke into a cold sweat looking at the revolver in his hand.

It wasn't like Nandu had never felt fear. He recalled the day a cobra had entered the house and sat coiled under the mattress. Nandu had feared for his life and that of his brothers. He also remembered the day his mother had gone into labour while giving birth to Balraj. Her screams could be heard from every room. Nandu had been so terrified that he had run into the field and stood there shivering for hours. He was petrified at the thought of losing his mother.

This feeling, as he held the revolver, was new and alien, yet it evoked a familiar sense of fear and nervousness. His chest heaved and his heart thudded loudly. His nostrils flared, as if gasping for the last strand of air. His palms were sweaty, and his brows had so much perspiration accumulated on them that his vision was blurred. It was winter, yet he felt as if he had been running under a hot summer sun for hours. Charles was telling him something about chambers, about .455 cartridges, but he could only register a muffled sound and see Charles's lips moving.

A moment later, Charles moved closer to Nandu and placed a hand on his shoulder. 'What is wrong, my boy? You seem to have lost your grip.'

'Sir,' Nandu finally whispered, 'will I have to kill someone with this … this thing?'

'As a soldier, I have had to kill many. After the first time, you get used to the idea. It only becomes easier after that. The target becomes prey, like the targets hanging on the wall, or that hay-stuffed effigy. You don't need to worry though. You are not a soldier, and you may not have to kill anyone, but you should be prepared to act in self-defence. Someday, you may need to defend yourself, and then you won't stand quietly in front of the killer, will you? In that moment, you will do everything to save yourself. Your mother's face, your sister's face and your brother's mischievous eyes will flash before you; you will do anything and everything to protect yourself, even if it means killing with your bare hands. I suggest that you not give it so much thought. Just consider it a task. Like when you make your rotis, you need to learn how to cook. You need that to survive, isn't that correct?

This is the same. You need to master this little black beauty so that it can protect you and your loved ones. Most young men from India already know how to wield these. They keep them hidden in their loincloths, looking for opportunities to kill one of us. And here we have willingly given you a weapon. Aren't you lucky, my boy? Very lucky, if you ask me!'

Charles's manner of speaking, referring to the basics of Nandu's day-to-day life, seemed to calm him down a bit. Nandu wiped the sweat off his brow and took a deep breath. He knew that there was nothing in this world that could stop him. He was intelligent and brave enough to master all that he needed to get to the next level in his training. He promised himself that this pistol would be the last of his hurdles, that he wouldn't let it overpower him.

He turned around and said, 'Thank you, you have made it very clear. I will practise day and night to get a grasp on it.'

'That is more like you, Nandlal. Once you are done for today, meet me in my office. I need to share some important news with you,' Charles said and turned around. He tugged at his belt braces and walked away.

Nandu, with the Webley in his hand, focused on the hay-stuffed human figure in front of him. He was determined to kill this monster, to pump all the bullets into its chest before the sun set.

Before long, Nandu was in Charles's office. Most days, Charles kept him standing while giving instructions, but that day he gestured for Nandu to sit. 'Do you want to have some tea, perhaps some cookies, Nandlal? I am famished. I didn't eat lunch properly. I was summoned by my supervisor. He wanted to talk about you.'

Nandu nodded. He liked the light-flavoured tea served in the cantonment. At home, it was a concoction of sugar and milk, with hardly any tea to taste. Charles rang a bell for the orderly and leaned towards Nandu. 'You understand that you are now prepared for action? We have trained you well. You received all-round training in combat and now in weapons, and a basic understanding of the human body. In a couple of months you will be well-equipped to defend yourself and, if needed, escape a tricky situation. I am very satisfied with your report. You may not have realized it, but we had our men following you everywhere. You were never seen with those revolutionary thugs. Instead, you were focused on what we had asked you to do. Now, my boy, you are going to get a taste of some action. Real action!'

When the tea was served, Nandu gingerly picked up a cookie, wondering where the conversation was heading.

'This thing you are eating is called a shortcake. Tell me, my boy, why is a biscuit called a shortcake? Is it short, is it creamy like a cake? Ah! So, you don't know. Well, you failed your first quiz,' Charles said and started laughing.

Nandu didn't find it funny. He was apprehensive about what was coming, but he managed to muster a smile. He focused on the fine bone china of the teacup in his hand. It was so different from the brass tumbler that his mother brought for him every morning, holding it with her much-soiled dupatta. Nandu placed a finger on the golden rim and admired the small pink flowers. *Someday, I will have a set like this of my own. Someday.*

Charles sensed Nandu's tension. He cleared his throat and leaned forward. 'Let me tell you about your first assignment, Nandlal. Things here are heating up. You know that. A group of young boys came to Firozpur recently, and their movements are suspicious. They hardly step out of their accommodation during the day and are seen scuttling in and out in the evenings. Now tell me, boy, why would a bunch of young lads your age *not* roam around and see the new city? Why would they not enjoy the scenic beauty of the Sutlej? Why would they sit at home the whole day? This is what I want you to find out. Who are they? Why are they here? What is their plan? I want every detail. The orderly will show you the house; it is close to the bazaar. You have four days to submit your report, all right?'

Nandu nodded. It seemed to be an easy assignment, and he intended to execute it well.

Charles straightened his back and said, 'After this assignment, you will be stationed in Amritsar. You will travel mid next month. There, you will work as a clerk in a newspaper press. I am calling it a press, but it is hardly one. It prints a tabloid twice a month, cheap stories about theatre and local bioscopes, etc. Its income is generated from printing pamphlets for small business owners, wedding cards, etc. The press is called New Horizon. I don't know which horizon it is a reference to, but the owner is a loyal man. He has sharp ears and eyes, which he puts to good use. He is a cunning fellow who enjoys the confidence of the revolutionaries.

They use his basement to print propaganda pamphlets. You will stay inside the press; in a room on the mezzanine floor. Well, it isn't a proper room, but it is good enough for one person. You will get thirty rupees a month. Your day job will be to gather news for the tabloid and to write and proofread the pamphlets. He will teach you how to take photographs, too. At times, he also covers the weddings and parties of the rich. In those cases, you will be the official photographer and reporter. Your prime responsibility will be to keep your eyes and ears open and to keep us informed. You will also gradually befriend the revolutionaries, win their confidence and report their movements. How you do it is up to you. You are trained and intelligent enough. Am I clear?'

'Yes, sir,' said Nandu, delighted at the prospect of moving to a big city and earning a handsome salary. He started calculating the amount he would send to his father to ease the situation at home. 'Sir, excuse me, how long will I be there? Is it a permanent job?'

'Nothing is permanent, my boy. I don't know how long you will be in Amritsar, or where your next station will be. I also follow orders, but I have overheard that it will be a couple of months, maybe more, and then you will be moved to Calcutta, which is a hotbed, filled with notorious criminals who pretend to be freedom fighters. Bollocks!'

Nandu thanked Charles and assured him that he was prepared to depart earlier than next month, if needed. But first, he had his new assignment to concentrate on.

Nandu was told to come back later to collect the introductory letter for the owner of the press, his address and other details. He was also told to pack his suitcase, and take the Webley pistol and the Morse code machine along.

Nandu cycled slowly to his house, thinking how to break the news to his family. He knew his mother would cry her heart out and sulk for days. He had to announce it fast so that not much fuss was created on the day of his departure. He had to meet his sister and Ajit, too. It would be hard to leave them behind. Nandu took his time as he made his way through the bazaar, taking in the sights and storing the images in his mind—the peepul tree, the Shiv mandir, the familiar faces of friends and neighbours. *Who knows when I will cycle home again on a wintry night? Who knows when someone will smile at me again and ask, 'Nandu Beta, all well at home?'*

4

On the first day of his first assignment, Nandu prayed to the gods before leaving home. He wanted to do well and impress Charles. He took leave from Lalaji, who was perhaps aware of the assignment but didn't say much.

An orderly took him to a building at the end of the bazaar. The area was relatively free from the usual hustle and bustle, even during the day. Though old and dilapidated, it housed two shops on the ground floor. One of them sold daily use items and hard-boiled sweets. The other was a tea stall that also offered fried savouries in the morning and evening. Nandu sat outside the stall, reading a newspaper and chatting with the customers. He pretended to be an unemployed youth who was staying in the vicinity and was scouting for a job.

Nandu stayed observant. While chatting with the tea stall owner, it was confirmed that a group of five boys in their early twenties was here from Calcutta. On the first day, Nandu didn't see them. The windows of the top floor, where they had taken two rooms, were tightly shut. The next evening, he spotted them going out. They returned with two big bags that seemed full. Nandu could see leafy vegetables on the top.

He couldn't help but think that it was a lot of vegetables for a few young lads. *Maybe they eat a lot.*

The next evening, the routine was repeated. Two or three boys went out for an hour after sunset and returned with large bags filled with vegetables. Nandu started preparing his report. There wasn't much to tell though. After all, one could not search or arrest someone for carrying food. Still, he kept up the vigilance.

Three days passed without anything worth mentioning. Nandu contemplated telling Charles that the assignment had hit a dead end. Perhaps it was just a group of boys who had chosen to travel this far in search of jobs. Maybe Firozpur had opportunities that their city lacked.

On the fourth day, as Nandu sat outside the stall, idly sipping on yet another cup of tea, there was a bang. One of the boys, bleeding profusely, rushed out. Two other boys rushed out after him, threw a large blanket on him, wrapped him in it and took him inside. One could hear the injured boy's loud moans. Nandu jumped on his cycle, rushed to the cantonment and headed straight to Charles's room.

Charles acted quickly. Almost immediately, the area was swarming with policemen. The house was raided. The boys were making crude bombs. Bags full of gunpowder and other items were found in abundance.

The boys were brutally beaten and then dragged out. Nandu noticed their eyes, full of loathing and defiance. Those eyes haunted him for a long time. As they were forcefully put into the police van, they turned around to look at him with aversion and hatred. Perhaps they knew that he had been instrumental in getting them caught. Something stirred inside him. Was he doing the right thing? The thought refused to leave his mind as he pedalled his way to the cantonment and then back home.

Charles was very happy with Nandu and his impeccable report. He couldn't stop praising him. Nandu tried to find out the fate of the arrested boys, but he was dismissed and asked to prepare for his journey to Amritsar. Nandu had a new task. He had to convince his parents to let him work in a different city.

Amidst the clattering of brass vessels, the slosh of dal in a bowl, Balraj belching and someone clicking their tongue while biting into sour pickle was not the right time to discuss any serious matter. Nandu refrained from bringing up his news during dinner. He waited for the house to quieten and then slowly headed to his parents' room. His mother was picking at a corn on her right toe, which had been bothering her for some time. His father sat on the bed, staring at nothing in particular.

Nandu coughed and asked for permission to enter. His mother was delighted. 'Come in, my son. I was thinking of calling you and showing you something, but I didn't want to disturb you. These days you work so hard. I can see how tired you are. And look at those dark circles. Tomorrow I will make a paste of dal and coconut oil for your face. That will take care of the rings around your eyes. Come inside, I have something to show you,' Prito said and rushed to her old trunk. She took out a muslin-covered packet and handed it to Nandu. 'Open it. This is for your bride. See how beautifully Rani Mausi has made the phulkari patterns. We stitched the sequins with silver and gold threads. Do you like it?'

Nandu opened it to reveal a beautiful red silk chaddar with flowers and gold work all over. It was shining under the night lamp. As he stood there holding it, the red colour seemed to change form. For a few seconds, he felt as if his hand was covered with warm blood. Was he hallucinating?

Nandu softly placed it on the bed and sat down on the edge of the bed. 'Bebe, it is beautiful, but I have something to share with you both. I have got a job in Amritsar. It is a good one, at a printing press, which will pay me thirty rupees a month. I need to leave by the end of this month. My marriage must wait, Bebe. I will surely marry the woman of your choice, but I need to work, see the world and earn some money.'

Prito stood quietly for a minute and then burst into tears. 'What world do you want to see? Is this not your world? Are we not a part of your world? You are breaking my heart. I have been dreaming of your marriage since the day you were born. Your Papaji and I are not getting younger. When will we play with our grandchildren? After our death? I have been saving money for your bride's clothes and a grand feast. Why do you have to go to some other city to earn? We don't need your money, or anything else. All we want is for you to live a happy life. Is that too much to ask?'

Papaji, who had been quiet all along, tried to soothe his wife. 'Please don't cry, Prito. The boy has a point. He needs to establish himself and earn a living. We must not become a hurdle in his dreams. Now tell me, Nandu, where is this job? What will it require you to do?'

Nandu told his father everything that Charles had told him, that he would be required to write and proofread pamphlets and also help with the printing. He also mentioned that he would get a room inside the press and a monthly salary of thirty rupees.

Prito sighed, folded the packet with the beautiful chaddar and kept it back inside the trunk. She wiped her tears and looked straight into Nandu's eyes. 'I suppose they are also giving you a mother to cook your meals. Good! Fewer rotis for me to make.' Saying this, she stormed out of the room.

Papaji put a hand on Nandu's shoulder. 'You know your mother. She gets angry when she is hurt. Give her a few days, and she will calm down. She loves her firstborn tremendously. Now that Geeta is married and gone, she clings to the three of you. I am happy for you. This is your age to see the world. I, too, wanted to visit the big cities, but I was married when I was sixteen. Then you and the others came along, and I forgot about my dreams. Go live your life, my son, but try to visit us as much as you can. This house will be so empty without you …' Papaji said in a choked voice.

Nandu couldn't control his tears. He rushed out of the room, stood under the mango tree and looked up at the sky. Once again, he felt torn between this world and the world that lay ahead of him. Once again, random thoughts crossed his mind. *Am I doing the right thing?*

The cool breeze brought little solace to his troubled mind. He never wanted his mother to be sad because of his decisions. He kept wondering what would make her happy. What could he do to make her smile again? He was clueless; his mind had gone blank.

Nandu's last few days in the village flew by. His mother kept packing and repacking his box, trying to stuff dry fruits, pickles, papadums, shirts, trousers and woollens into it. At times, frustrated, she would sit on the edge of the bed and cry. Then, looking up towards heaven, she would talk to her deity. 'Why did I have to see this day? Why didn't you call me to heaven, to my mother and mother-in-law? Why did I give birth to a boy who would never listen to me? Hai Rabba!'

Nandu left her alone when she began her monologue with God, slipping away while she waited for God to answer her questions.

Closer to the day of his departure, Charles briefed Nandu and gave him the address and contact details he would need in Amritsar. From the station, he was to go straight to Sachindra Sharma, the owner of New Horizon Printing Press*. All arrangements had been made. He was also given an advance of thirty rupees, which would be adjusted against his salary, to ensure he settled down easily in the new city.

Having advised Nandu, Charles got up from his chair and shook his hand firmly. 'Make me proud, my boy, make me proud. You are my protégé. I know you will do a good job and the British Raj will reward you amply. You are beginning a new life. I wish you the best.'

Nandu, feeling emotional, nearly bent down to touch Charles's feet, but then he quickly checked himself as this was not the custom of the sahibs. He tucked in all the papers with the information into the pocket of his trousers. He planned to write it all down in his notebook once he was back home. He never trusted scraps of paper.

Nandu also went to meet Lalaji who had already been briefed by the cantonment. He was happy for Nandu and pushed ten rupees into his palm. 'Go, boy, buy a decent pair of shoes and a shirt. These thin slippers of yours will not survive the journey. Also, now you are going to stay in a big city, so you must dress appropriately. I will meet you when I come to Amritsar to pick up merchandise. I will inform your parents before coming, so that they can send some goodies. I am sure you will miss home-cooked food. You may travel the whole world, but you will never get your mother's love and her food anywhere. Trust me, I have seen quite a bit of life.'

Nandu sat with Lalaji for a while, sipping milk tea and chatting about the political scenario and mayhem unfolding across the country. Before leaving, Nandu turned around and stood for a few minutes, trying to soak in every detail. Lalaji watched him and smiled.

Nandu also went to meet his sister. She was emotional about letting her elder brother go, and the fact that he would not be around when her baby was born in a few months. They sat together recollecting happy memories. His brother-in-law gave him a few names and addresses of friends in Amritsar. A while later, Nandu bid farewell to them.

For the next two days, he roamed around with Ajit. They drank endless cups of tea and ate countless samosas. They visited the old ruins behind the gurdwara and near the pond. They spoke about their school days, their Hindi teacher, their crushes in the neighbourhood and all the mischief that had led their fathers to break canes on their backs. It was as if time had paused and taken the two friends back to a carefree life.

Ajit was still unsure of his future. His father was a wealthy landlord with hundreds of acres to his name. Ajit could opt to look after the accounts and lead a comfortable life, but he was inspired by his friend to do more. Nandu told him that once he had spent some time in Amritsar, he might be able to find a lucrative job there for his friend.

Ajit was excited at the prospect of being with his friend once more. He rubbed his hands together and said, 'It will be fun. We will go to the cinemas and check out the city girls. Who knows, we may even bump into Asha!'

When the friends finally said goodbye, Ajit promised to accompany Nandu to the railway station.

The day arrived. Papaji came into Nandu's room very early in the morning, which he usually didn't. He had a brown paper packet under his arm. Nandu sat up.

Papaji cleared his throat and said, 'I am not a rich father, or else my son would not have to travel far to earn thirty rupees a month. He would be preparing to go to a college in the city or abroad. I couldn't give you much, but here is a gift from me. It is a coat. It may not be the best or latest cut, but it will keep you warm. Whenever you wear it, you will feel our arms around you. I hope you like it. It is brown and will match your trousers and shirts.'

Nandu was moved. He touched his father's feet, opened the packet and tried the coat on. His mother walked in with a handful of dry chillis, which she waved over his head to ward off the evil eye.

At the time of departure, there was more crying. The neighbours peeped in; people pushed boxes of sweets into Nandu's hand. For the hundredth time, he was reminded to keep his tickets and money safe, that big cities were filled with thieves, and that he should eat on time and stay warm.

Nandu's heart was too heavy to disagree or answer, so he merely nodded. His mother refused to come out of her room and kept sobbing into her dupatta. Nandu hugged his father. He bent to touch both his parents' feet, but his mother moved her feet away, expressing her displeasure.

Dhyanchand and Ajit accompanied Nandu to the railway station. He turned around to look at the place where he had grown up. Barring some nearby villages, he had never undertaken such a long journey alone. He was nervous and sad, but also excited for the new life that beckoned. He boarded the train and waved to his friend and brother.

The train hissed ferociously. The station was shrouded in thick black smoke, as if obliterating Nandu's past and drawing a line to indicate what he was leaving behind.

AMRITSAR

5

Nandu was happy with his window seat on the train. He could not only enjoy the scenic view, but also turn his face towards the window when tears overwhelmed him. However, by the time the train crossed the second station, the coal dust had started burning his eyes. As he rubbed his eyes, many thoughts crossed his mind. He worried about his parents, his sister, the farmland and his friend. He was anxious about what the world held for him and where this journey was leading him.

Consciously, he turned his thoughts towards the city that was going to be his home for some time. He softly said the word 'Amritsar' twice. He liked the sound of it; there was something sweet about it. It dawned on him that the name of the city literally meant 'the holy tank surrounding the nectar of immortality'. The city was named after the pond that surrounded the gurdwara there. His mother had talked about their visit to Amritsar when Nandu had been just a baby. He was barely twelve or thirteen years old when the Jallianwala Bagh massacre took place. The whole of Punjab had been on red alert. There were protests and killings everywhere. Nandu remembered how no one was allowed to go out in the evenings, that he had to play alone in the courtyard. He recalled the elders discussing the incident and its potential fallout while he stood near the door, straining his ears to catch what they were saying.

Ever since, Amritsar was considered a hotbed for revolutionary activities by the British. His mother had told him to visit the gurdwara, which he intended to do, but he was more eager to pay homage to the martyrs of Jallianwala Bagh. No Britisher could stop him from doing so.

Charles had told Nandu to find out more about the socialist party that operated through sleeper cells in the city. Youth drawn towards revolution, from various parts of the country, used Amritsar as a meeting point.

Nandu wondered if he would be able to nullify the fervour of the young revolutionaries. Somewhere deep down he, too, realized that their cause was just. Thoughts like these made him restless. All he wanted to do was to enjoy this journey.

Nandu was happy when a family of five, including an infant, came and sat with him. The Kohli family—comprising of elderly parents, a son, daughter-in-law and a baby who was not more than two years old—had gone to their ancestral home to attend a wedding. The father had a stationery shop in Amritsar, and the son was a school teacher. The mother complained of arthritis, and the harried daughter-in-law tried in vain to hush the bawling baby who was scared by the train's rattling.

The family warmed up to Nandu quickly. The son, Pradeep, talked incessantly about the city, his job and their tiny two-room apartment. The father admitted that he never felt like going back to the city after visiting the open fields, breathing the clean air and eating the fresh produce from the fields. He intended to sell his shop and go back to the village in a few years. The atmosphere in the city was not getting better, he told Nandu, adding that every month there were killings, protest marches and lathi-charges. There had been a couple of wounded revolutionaries trying to hide in his shop, which had led to police searches.

Pradeep warned Nandu. 'Stay away from protest marches. If you do get caught in them, look for a shop or house where you can take refuge. The police are merciless. They open fire or start beating indiscriminately. They leave you wounded and bleeding, or they put you into a prison van and take you somewhere. Most people never return. It is better to steer clear of these things if you are going to the city to earn a living and send money home.'

Nandu assured him that he would confine himself to the press and venture out only to eat or buy necessary items. The mother kindly invited him to their house whenever he wanted to eat home-cooked food.

The Kohlis were carrying sweets and savouries, which they gladly shared with Nandu. Pradeep and Nandu bought tea for everyone. The journey was quite pleasant, except for the crying baby who ultimately fell asleep in his mother's lap.

When the train pulled into the station, Pradeep offered Nandu a ride in their tonga. He explained that with the baby and his mother's gout, they would have to hire one anyway, and that Nandu could squeeze in the front with him. 'You have just one suitcase, which you might have to keep on your lap. It will be a bit uncomfortable, but at least you won't have to walk alone in the dark. From where we drop you, walk straight for ten minutes and you will arrive at the junction near your destination. Is that all right?' Pradeep asked.

It was more than all right for Nandu, who was worried about getting to the press. He accepted the offer and apologized to the family several times for the inconvenience. As he got off the tonga, the mother again invited Nandu to their house.

Nandu took the blessings of the parents, shook hands with Pradeep, touched the sleeping baby's face lightly and started to walk towards his destination.

Pradeep's directions were precise. Minutes later, Nandu found himself at a T-junction. The press was a short distance away, on the left. It looked quite dilapidated and in need of a coat of paint. A tangled mass of electric wires hung precariously on top of the iron grill gate that was rusting in places. Nandu entered and made his way to the first floor using a wooden staircase that creaked under his feet.

Sachindra Sharma* was a thin, insignificant-looking man who wore spectacles. He was sitting behind a table with some papers in front of him. Nandu looked at the suspenders holding up his trousers and assumed that Sharmaji, which was what he had decided to call him, had probably lost a lot of weight.

Sharmaji got up and shook Nandu's hand. 'Was your train late? I was getting worried. I must go home now. My little one has a fever, and this part of the town is not very safe after dark. I have a cycle, still it takes me almost an hour to reach home.'

Nandu realized that Sharmaji liked to talk without giving anyone a chance to respond.

Sharmaji took Nandu to the mezzanine floor, to his tiny room. He left after instructing Nandu to lock the gate every night. Nandu was alone in the musty room that smelt of carbon and ink. It was his first night without his family and friends, in a city that he knew nothing about.

Slowly, Nandu's eyes adjusted to the poor light. His abode for the next few months, or until he received instructions to move, was so small that it felt as if the walls would close in on him. There was a bed—a plank of wood supported by four legs—in the middle of the room, with a thin mattress, a much-stained pillow and a blanket. It wasn't big enough for Nandu's large frame, but he would have to manage. The walls were probably yellow, but the paint had peeled off in several places and displayed signs of seepage. A large calendar hung on one of the walls with the name of the press and Lord Shiva's face on it, adding a little colour to the drab surroundings.

In one corner was a tin table with a small stove, basic utensils and some spoons and teacups. Sharmaji had already warned him not to do any cooking to prevent a fire. The stove was to be used only for making tea and warming up food bought from the nearby shop. There was also a tiny wooden cupboard with three empty shelves. Nandu was too exhausted to unpack. He decided to live out of his suitcase for the time being.

It was nearly ten at night. Nandu's stomach was growling. He opened the steel case he was carrying. The aroma of the food his mother had cooked for him filled the room. As he sat on the edge of the bed and ate, he felt alone and desolate. He tried to imagine what his family was doing. Perhaps they were sleeping peacefully with the light breeze wafting in through the windows, bearing the smell of flowers from their garden. Again, he wondered whether he was doing the right thing by leaving behind a world of love and comfort to chase an unknown dream.

As his eyes closed from sheer exhaustion, Nandu left the food in the box half-eaten and curled up on the narrow bed. He tried to rest his body and mind, praying that the next day would be better and bring some hope with it.

Nandu woke up early after a restless night. He was used to sleeping on his charpoy under the mango tree and waking up to birds chirping. He went to the toilet downstairs to freshen up before Sharmaji arrived and made a cup of tea to have with the leftover food. He felt more positive, probably because of the cold water that had washed away some of his apprehensions. He was ready for a new beginning.

Sharmaji arrived at ten in the morning. After cursory prayers to his deity, an idol kept on a shelf behind him, he started explaining the work to Nandu.

Nandu was to proofread everything that went for printing and maintain an account of payments received and payouts. He also had to look after the monthly salaries of the five workers who were slowly coming in. Nandu was introduced as the new manager of the press, who had come highly recommended by the British at the cantonment in Firozpur.

In the afternoon, Sharmaji urged Nandu to accompany him to an eatery, gesturing that there were confidential things that could not be discussed in the office. Nandu understood and got up.

Sharmaji explained to Nandu that it was best to order the vegetable platter as it was affordable and wholesome. He could order eggs or meat occasionally, but that was sure to pinch his pocket. Sharmaji also introduced Nandu to the owner of the eatery, saying that he would come regularly.

The food was indeed delicious. The platter included roti, rice, lentils, two vegetable dishes and a small bowl of dessert, all of which were tasty and reasonably priced.

Sharmaji smiled and said, 'If the owner feels generous, he may give you extra puris and gajar ka halwa, but that is only when winter is ending, and the horses refuse to eat radish and carrots anymore.'

Nandu liked his employer's sense of humour.

Sharmaji ordered two cups of tea after their meal and pulled his chair closer to Nandu's. 'I usually don't have tea after a meal, but today I need to discuss the important thing that has brought you here. Your main job.' He inched even closer and lowered his voice further. Sharmaji who was also a British informer started to speak. 'The revolutionaries come to the press thrice a week. On Tuesdays, Thursdays and Saturdays. I call them revolutionaries, but they are just university and college students, as young as you. They are more passionate than ever and ready to take extreme measures to fulfil their mission. Of late, they have been busy printing their fortnightly tabloid *Kesariya Kranti**, also called KK. It is in Gurmukhi script, and I am the only one who can give them the typesetting they want. They want to expose the corrupt British Raj and the funds that are being embezzled to England. They have moles in the revenue service who give them information. Their news is backed by evidence; it is not fake. Apart from that, they occasionally print pamphlets calling for the boycott of British goods, and protest marches and gatherings. They distribute these through street urchins. Your prime responsibility will be to befriend them and regularly send the matter they print to the cantonment, with correct translations. I suspect they are planning something big soon, which you have to find out. They are young, educated, and suspicious, so they will not allow you to be a part of their inner circle easily. Your impressive appearance might help to an extent, but gaining their confidence won't be easy. Your people skills are good, and you have an air of innocence that you must use to your advantage.'

Nandu assured Sharmaji that he would do his best, and that he had been trained to work with discretion.

Both of them got up. Nandu tipped the head waiter, who was hovering around, a few paisa. Delighted, he told Nandu, 'We start cooking at seven in the evening. Try to come around that time; the food is fresh and hot.'

Nandu nodded and headed back to the press with Sharmaji.

6

Sure enough, becoming a part of the revolutionaries' group was not easy. In the evening, after work and a quick bite at the eatery, Nandu would hang around in the press, pretending to check some copies and write a few lines. None of these tasks were essential, but they gave him a reason to be there. Initially, the revolutionaries completely ignored him. They were a busy lot. Done with college for the day, they would get to work immediately. There were five of them, two women and three men.

Madhav gave instructions to everyone. He was a student of law and came from a family of well-established lawyers. He was arrogant and proud of his lineage.

Vimla* was a petite woman who had just started college after completing her matriculation. She came from a family of doctors. Her brother had been sent abroad to study medicine, but she was denied that privilege because she was a girl. She had a mind of her own and was quite set in her ways. Madhav and she had known each other since childhood.

Amita was a primary school teacher who supported her ailing parents and young siblings. Well past the marriageable age, she had come to terms with the fact that her plain looks and the burden of responsibilities did not make her a sought-after bride.

Virendra was the son of a storekeeper. He manned his father's shop during the day. He wanted to rise above the ordinary, and fighting for the freedom of his country was his path to martyrdom.

Ali's family manned eateries at the old chowk. He was the quiet one who followed orders diligently. He was also the youngest, barely in his twenties.

All of them came into the press quietly and spoke in hushed tones, as if someone was eavesdropping. They would finish everything in an hour or two and leave as quietly as they had come. Madhav wrote the pamphlets, read them out and helped the others with the printing. Sometimes they sat and discussed their operations. Although they worked independently, they were a part of the larger socialist party and would join it on the days they didn't come to the press. Nandu was yet to identify their headquarters and leaders.

A few days ago, Madhav had come into the press in the evening, quite agitated. He gathered everyone and held up the newspaper he had in his hand. 'Jallianwala Bagh is not new, my dear friends. It is never new. Oh! How many times do we have to shed our blood to satisfy our masters? How much blood will quench their thirst?'

Vimla pushed a stool towards him and asked, 'What happened, Madhav? What do you have in your hand?'

Madhav cleared his throat. 'Do you remember the Ajnala incident during the 1857 uprising? Two hundred and eighty-two sepoys were killed and dumped into a well. Giani Hira

Singh Dard wrote about it in his magazine *Phulwari*. Today, *Fansi Ank* from Allahabad has carried the news. They have mentioned the first-hand account of an eyewitness, Baba Jagat Singh. Babaji is almost a hundred years old. He was present that day when his partners were killed. Oh! How horrific it must have been for him to keep remembering that one incident all through the years.'

Gathering some courage, Nandu stepped closer to them.

Madhav asked him sarcastically, 'Clerk Babu, what brings you to our humble abode?'

Nandu was irritated with the tone, but he had been trained to control his temper. He replied politely, 'I was wondering if I can be of any help. I work and stay here, and it gets rather lonely upstairs in my room. I may be useful to you.'

'And how do you intend to make yourself useful, Clerk Babu?'

'I am not "Clerk Babu". My name is Nandlal, and you can call me Nandu. I do the proofreading, printing and writing here. I can help with all of this if you want. I see that you print a tabloid, and I have a working knowledge of English, Gurmukhi and Hindi. To start with, I can make tea for all of you.'

Madhav softened a bit. 'That is a good proposition. A cup of tea would be nice, and then we can see if you will be of help to us or not.'

Nandu noticed that he had caught Vimla's attention. He wondered why. Vimla was fair and tall with a long braid and a pair of glasses sitting on her long nose, which she kept adjusting. Each time she raised her hand to coil her braid into a bun, something fluttered inside Nandu's heart. It was an unfamiliar sensation, nothing like what Ajit and he had experienced looking at Asha. Nandu liked to keep looking at Vimla, which she had noticed. Whenever their eyes met, she would hurriedly look away and pretend to be busy.

Now Vimla spoke to him for the first time, her voice soft with a musical lilt. 'Where do you make tea? Let me help. I am sure it is not easy to make so many cups by yourself.'

Nandu was grateful to be alone with her. He showed her the way up to his tiny room and the old kerosene stove. Vimla deftly put the water to boil and added measured spoons of tea and sugar and poured the milk. Nandu kept staring at her neck, at the trickle of sweat that made its way down, the rhythmic tinkling of her bangles as she stirred the tea.

'Can you help me carry the cups down?' she asked suddenly.

Nandu came back to his senses and blushed. 'Yes, of course. You go down and I will bring them. The staircase is too narrow for two people.'

That was the beginning of Nandu's entry into the group.

At first, they asked him to proofread pamphlets, which were generally about a protest march or speech. The tabloid that was published covered news about corruption in the existing government, rising food prices, people dying of hunger and farmers committing suicide due to unpaid loans.

Nandu was curious about how they got their hands on government documents, especially their sources in the revenue department. He always ensured to keep aside a copy of each tabloid, which he diligently translated and sent to Charles.

Nearly three months had passed since Nandu came to Amritsar. He had started sending extra money home, so that his father could begin repairing the house before the monsoon arrived. His sister, Geeta, had had a son, and Ajit was to be married soon. He was urging Nandu to come home for the wedding and refused to visit the bride's house until his friend was there.

In these three months, Nandu and Vimla's friendship had blossomed. They often talked while laying the plates for the snacks that Nandu occasionally brought back from the eatery.

One lazy Sunday afternoon, when Nandu was propped up on his bed, reading a book, he heard a knock on the door and was surprised to see Vimla standing there. She looked exceedingly pretty, dressed in a floral print salwar-kameez and with her hair open. For a few seconds, Nandu kept staring at her until she said that she had left some important documents behind.

After a while, they both sat down to drink tea. Vimla looked up and said softly, 'Have you ever thought of joining us? I know you help us a lot, but that is as an outsider. I... I mean we ... all of us would be very happy if you joined us.'

'I have responsibilities back home, people who wait for the money I earn, Vimla.'

'I am not asking you to give up your job but think of the country. Do you know how many people die of hunger on the streets because our wealth and produce are being shipped to England? Don't you feel angry?'

The conversation carried on for some more time. Finally, Nandu asked, 'Do you think that we can achieve independence, that one day our country will be free of poverty and everyone will be treated equally?'

Vimla raised her arched eyebrows and looked directly at Nandu. 'I am a dreamer, and there is no harm in dreaming and trying to realize those dreams. That is why I am sitting here today with you, in an empty press.'

Nandu asked her to explain.

In response, she stood up, tied her hair and walked towards the door. Looking back, she said, 'Someday, you will understand. Maybe now is not the time.' With a smile, she left.

Nandu couldn't sleep that night. He kept wondering what Vimla had meant. He had befriended the revolutionaries to spy on them and send information to Charles, but he was getting attached to them. The news of young people like him dying in hundreds, languishing in jails, and the eyes of those he had helped the police catch in Firozpur still haunted him. Could he not earn his thirty rupees, fulfil his dreams and yet help his country? He was looking for a middle path.

Nandu started meeting Vimla frequently, but always inside the press. Some days Vimla came early, some days she came unexpectedly. They sat and spoke, shared a meal and began enjoying each other's company. A bond had started forming.

One evening, when she arrived, Vimla looked harrowed. She was being pressured by her family to get married. 'I can avoid the discussion of my marriage till I graduate, but who knows after that. I won't, at any cost. My life is dedicated to my country, my motherland. I am planning to escape. I have a cousin in Calcutta; she is the only one I can confide in,' she told Nandu.

Nandu wanted to soothe her, to put an arm around her, but he hesitated. 'Don't worry, things will sort out on their own.'

Vimla moved closer to him and rested her head on his broad shoulder. Nandu touched her lightly. A shiver ran down his spine. He had never felt like this. Nandu wanted the clock to stop so that they could sit in this embrace forever, their bodies touching lightly, comforting each other. Nandu realized that he had started to think of a life with her, and if that meant accompanying her on her path, he was willing to do that. He could not think of living without Vimla any longer. She was in his dreams, and he sensed her presence even when she was not around. He waited to see her each evening, to hear her voice, to be next to her, to have a cup of tea with her. Nandu knew he was in love.

As time went by Nandu became deeply entrenched with the revolutionaries. He advised them and worked with them, helping them in any way he could. However, he remained cognizant of the fact that he was working for the British government. He regularly collected information on protest marches, gatherings and any other unrest and diligently updated the cantonment. Nandu was torn between two lives—the one he had opted for and the one that was coming towards him. One life had duties and responsibilities and the other had Vimla.

Nandu wanted to do something big so that Vimla and her group would admire him. Something that would help the cause and the fight for freedom. Soon, an opportunity presented itself. Nandu decided to seize it. He was not very bothered about the consequences; his aim was to avoid getting caught and charged with treason.

Before he embarked on this mission, he borrowed an advance from Sharmaji and sent it home. In case something happened to him, at least he would have paid for the repair of the house and kept his promise to his father. The fields had delivered a good yield this season, so money was not an issue anymore. He was fighting the yearning to see his family once more, but it was not the right time. What he was about to do could put everyone in danger, including his tiny nephew whom he had only seen in a photograph.

Lord Ranbir Singh Sodhi* was one of the richest men in Amritsar with several factories and a finger in every pie: construction, steel, oil mills, cinema halls and whatnot.

His success was also thanks to his ability to keep everyone happy. While he was close to the Indian National Congress and its leaders, he was equally close to the British government. Rumour had it that he kept those he needed on his payroll and doled out favours to people in positions of power.

In ten days, he was expected to announce the engagement of his eldest daughter to an Oxford-returned youth who was to join the court as a barrister. Sodhi was not shy of spending money. He was throwing a lavish party to introduce his would-be son-in-law into the elite circle. The grapevine was abuzz with rumours of nautch girls being brought over from Lucknow and of the best chefs being hired from the various residencies and countless barrels of foreign alcohol being bought for the event. Sharmaji's press had received a sizeable portion of the business, starting from printing the invitation letter in gold lettering to the menu and name cards at the tables.

Nandu was to ensure that everything was in order. He began formulating a plan that would use this opportunity to the advantage of his new friends. The following evening, after poring over copies and corrections, he met his friends in the basement, where they were busy debating the dates of a protest march and the contents of a pamphlet.

Nandu pulled up a chair. 'How long will you walk on the streets of the city, shouting a few slogans and thinking that you are making a dent in the freedom movement? Don't you think it is time to shake the tree, or maybe attempt to uproot it?' he said slowly.

'What exactly do you have in mind, Clerk Babu? Cough it up, spit it out, but in a different direction. It's as if we have nothing better to do but listen to an amateur, a child, a toddler who has still not taken his first step in the freedom movement,' Madhav retorted.

Vimla came to Nandu's rescue. 'Madhav, why are you so harsh with him? All he tries to do is help us. Is there any harm in listening to him?'

'Okay, my lady. Shoot, Clerk Babu.'

Nandu briefed the group about the upcoming celebration and showed them the copies he had. Then, bending forward, he whispered, 'There will be many lords and ladies, and the judge himself. It is not easy to manage so many people, especially when there is so much food, wine and music. Many will go unnoticed, especially the waiters and other staff serving food. This is your chance to finish off your target, I mean, kill them. You have the means, you have the intention, and now you have the opportunity. You just need to be sure of your target from the list of invitees.'

Everyone liked the plan. They also agreed that each detail had to be worked out. Nothing could be left to chance. A couple of evenings were spent working out every aspect of the impending assault—what was feasible, what could be potentially dangerous and what was too far-fetched to accomplish. Everything was thrashed out after heated arguments and debates. The plan gained momentum as the day of the celebration approached.

It was decided that when Nandu went to deliver the printed material for the party, he would take a good look around and prepare a rough plan. Vimla and Madhav had visited the house with their parents as they knew the Sodhi family, which was why they were ruled out from being a part of the operation. Virendra knew the caterer who was sending the dry fruits and decoration material. He planned to try and secure part-time work for Ali and himself for that day as waiters or overseers in the kitchen. Two pistols were procured from leaders of the socialist party. It was decided that the pistols would be kept hidden in Nandu's room because no one, not even a maid, came there. After a heated and anxious discussion, all of them departed chanting 'Vande Mataram' in hushed tones.

On the designated day, Nandu went to Sodhi's house. A low-ranking clerk who worked for Sodhi met him. As he walked from the gate to the office, he made a note of the surroundings. Down the corridor was the banquet hall where guests were usually entertained. On the pretext of using the washroom, he identified the door that led to the kitchen and the barbeque area. Outside, workers were already polishing brass items and varnishing wood. Nandu walked around unnoticed as he tried to figure out the layout of the house. He had no means of going upstairs where the family lived, but that was not required as all guests would be in the large hall on the ground floor. Satisfied that he could draw a rough sketch, he quietly left the house.

Later, he shared the list of guests and the name cards with his friends. Every person's background and rank in the British government was assessed.

Madhav said, 'This is the chance of a lifetime. We don't know what the future holds for us. Let us make the judge our target. If we can kill him, it will make enough noise to shake the core of the British government.'

Ultimately, after much debate, it was decided that the judge would be the target. He was likely to be the most sought-after man that day, most likely to be surrounded by people and security.

The evening before the party, all details were reviewed and last-minute checks were done. Virendra and Ali would carry the pistols, which the gardener—one of their own—had agreed to conceal. The other group members would go into hiding, as would Virendra and Ali once the job was completed. Everyone knew that their chances of making it out were slim. They were likely to be killed on the spot. Their target, the judge, would come in his vehicle with his guards. He would be ambushed in the garden. The group had decided that there would be no communication between them for a month. They planned to re-emerge a month later, once things settled down.

As everyone prepared, Vimla and Nandu went up to his room without anyone noticing. Vimla rested her hands on the table where she often made tea. 'So, this is how we end. Our journey together was short but unforgettable,' she said as her thin, tall frame shook with an uncontrollable sob. She hid her face in her palms.

Nandu pulled her to his chest and they stood locked in an embrace for long, tears streaming down their cheeks. They didn't want to let go.

Finally, Vimla spoke. 'Where will you go? Have you decided? They are sure to come after you, too.'

'No, I haven't planned. Going back to the village will put everyone in danger. I might disappear, but I haven't given it thought. Have you decided?'

'Yes, I will go to my cousin in Calcutta. I can't tell you the address because if you are caught, they have ways of extracting information from you. If you happen to be there and join the group, you will surely find me. Please, Nandu, try to locate me. I will wait.'

Nandu clasped her face and kissed her for the first time. The sweetness of her breath and the softness of her lips remained with him for the rest of his life. His first kiss had a lingering effect on him. Vimla remained his first love forever.

After the group left, there was an eerie silence in the press. The only sound was that of Nandu's feet and the creaking of the old staircase. Nandu sat on the edge of the bed. An inertia took over him. He kept staring at the wall in front of him, clasping his hands together. He couldn't get Vimla out of his mind. For the first time, he experienced a burning desire for a woman. The feeling was overwhelming. He got up to get himself some water to drink. A lot of thoughts were weighing on his mind: the impending plan and its consequences, what if he got caught, what if Vimla got caught, what if his house in the village was raided. There were many ifs but no answers.

Nandu slept fitfully that night. He dreamt of fleeing from a monster that was clutching Vimla, that she was slowly getting sucked into quicksand. He woke up sweating profusely, his heart racing. A cool shower calmed him down.

The next day, he pretended to go about his routine as usual. He even visited the eatery, but the food felt tasteless. He somehow managed to gulp a few bites.

In the evening, he kept looking at the big wall clock, but time refused to move forward. There was nothing that he could do anymore. He couldn't even go anywhere to gather news of what was happening. Neither could he ask anyone. He decided to go to bed early. Perhaps a good night's sleep would help.

He woke up with a jolt. Someone was knocking violently and rattling the iron gate. He ran downstairs to see Sharmaji panting and heaving. Nandu noticed he was shaking. He offered Sharmaji a glass of water.

Sitting down with a thud, and a bit calmer, Sharmaji told Nandu, 'A disaster has happened. There has been a shootout at the function. I don't have the details, but apparently, while the nautch girls were dancing, the judge's car was leaving the premises. A waiter broke all barriers, shouted "Vande Mataram" and shot at the car. He was killed immediately by the guards. One of his accomplices was taken into custody. The judge was not in the car. It was a junior-ranking officer called McCauley* and his wife. She was heavily pregnant and not feeling well so the judge offered his car to take them home. McCauley is gravely injured, but his wife died on the spot, as did their child. The sahibs are enraged and have placed every Indian present at the function under house arrest. They will soon start a combing operation and issue a curfew. I am fleeing with my family to the village in an hour.

So should you. We might also come under suspicion as the cards were printed here. I suggest you pack your belongings and leave for Delhi immediately. Go to my relative's house. There is a train in less than an hour. Hurry up, get going!'

Nandu rushed. He just had a few clothes to pack, which he threw into a trunk and ran down to where Sharmaji was waiting. They hugged each other and promised to be in touch, if possible. Lights were quickly switched off and the iron gate was locked.

Nandu paused to look at the building that had been his home in the city, then rushed away. There was no time left for contemplation. He ran towards the station with his trunk, hoping to make it on time. The train was delayed by a few minutes, so he found a wooden chair and sat down. He looked at the address that Sharmaji had given. It was his brother-in-law's house, where Nandu could stay until he knew what his next assignment was.

Suddenly, through the smoke and mist, he saw a familiar figure. It was Madhav. He came running towards Nandu and embraced him. 'We shook the empire, thanks to you, my dearest brother. Sorry, I underestimated you. I am glad that you are leaving, too, or they would have arrested you and tortured you into confessing. They are closing all roads leading to Amritsar and will soon issue a curfew. All police stations have been alerted, and people are being arrested indiscriminately. I am taking Vimla to Calcutta and will hide there for a while. We will be in the New Market area. If you happen to be there, and if destiny wishes, we will meet again.

So long, my friend. Vande Bharat, Vande Mataram,' Madhav said and left as quickly as he had come.

Nandu craned his neck to see if he could catch a glimpse of Vimla. For a moment, he thought he saw her sitting by a window, her beautiful eyes looking forlorn. The thought of not being able to see her again surpassed all other apprehensions. As he boarded the crowded train to Delhi and squatted on the floor with others, dog-tired, he bid goodbye to Amritsar, taking all the memories away with him. Perhaps it was forever.

DELHI

7

In Delhi the next morning, Nandu headed to Sachindra Sharma's brother-in-law's house in Chandni Chowk. The dingy lane leading up to it was neither welcoming nor pleasant to the sensory organs. The roads were overflowing with sewage and the area, in general, was overcrowded with makeshift food stalls and people selling their wares in baskets. Nandu had to navigate several meandering lanes to get there.

It was a chaotic and noisy household of four brothers, their wives, children and grandparents. The house itself was old, with several rooms and a courtyard that was shared between all the families. Nandu was given a tiny room at the end of a long corridor. The women of the household were not happy to cook for an unknown stranger, but they never voiced it. Every day, he was called for three meals in the space adjacent to the kitchen, where the rest of the male members lined up to sit on the floor and eat.

After two days, Nandu contacted Charles. He had to hear a mouthful about not intercepting the incident, and his departure to Delhi was also questioned. Nandu lined up a series of excuses that satisfied Charles, but he was not pleased about Nandu fleeing to Delhi without consulting him. This lapse, however, was excused because of Nandu's earlier diligence.

The British government had left no stone unturned to catch the masterminds of the incident in Amritsar, but they had not been successful. The person who had been captured was tortured and had died in jail without divulging any information. Since the group in question's activities and history were being combed, Nandu, too, was told to stay alert as the British knew that the group frequented the printing press. Nandu's heart sank at the news that Virendra had become a martyr. His thoughts went back to the evenings of endless cups of tea and sarcastic banter.

Charles informed Nandu that his next destination was Calcutta. He was to reach the city in a few days and work with a silk trader who had Burmese connections and was friendly with the Chinese and Japanese immigrants there. Nandu's tickets, details of accommodation and an introductory letter were expected soon. His work was the same—gathering intelligence—but he was warned that Calcutta would be far more challenging. It was known as the hotbed of revolutionary activities with youth from Dhaka and other parts of the country coming together there.

Nandu had some time to explore Delhi. He went to see the Qutab Minar, Red Fort and Purana Qila. He wished his family was with him. They did not even know that he had left Amritsar. Nandu knew they would only get worried and keep writing to him. He also missed Vimla terribly and thought about her a lot, wondering where she was and whether she thought about him. He just wanted to sit close to her and experience the bliss of basking in her soft glow, just the way he had in Amritsar.

In Chandni Chowk, the men of the household were very friendly. They would invite Nandu to join their discussions about work, price rise and general politics. Nandu often took sweets and savouries for them, as a gesture to thank them for their hospitality.

Finally, Nandu received his instructions and tickets for Calcutta. Another long train journey awaited him. He knew the language spoken there would be different. Hindi might work, but Nandu planned to learn Bengali soon. He would need it if he was to become a part of the revolutionaries. He informed his hosts that he would leave in two days.

The evening before his departure, while Nandu was busy packing, the youngest nephew ran into his room and told him that two men had come to meet him. Nandu was perplexed. He knew no one in Delhi except his hosts. With the little boy tugging at his shirt, Nandu headed out to see the visitors. He was apprehensive. Was it the secret police?

At the main door, he saw two young boys barely out of their teens. They introduced themselves as brothers and told him in a hushed tone that he should be in Rabri Bhandar, a popular eatery near Gole Market, in exactly two hours. Nandu remembered visiting the plain-looking shop that sold sweets, tea and savouries but was best known for its freshly fried evening snacks that sold like hot cakes.

The mysterious message rang alarm bells in his mind. *Is this a trap? Have the British found out? Is the combing operation still active? Have they succeeded in locating the revolutionaries?*

The boys refused to divulge any more and simply asked him to be present at the designated time and place.

Nandu was in two minds. Should he go to the shop, or should he quietly leave the city as per plan? His heart was thumping in his chest. *What if I get caught? What if I am thrown into some obscure jail and tortured to confess about the plan and the names of those involved?* He would never give away Vimla's name. Never. *Will they kill me? Will I ever see my parents again?*

Curiosity got the better of him, and he decided to go. He took a little money and informed the eldest brother that he was heading out to have a last look around Delhi and would be back in a couple of hours.

A while later, as he waited in a corner at the shop, he ordered some sweets to be packed and a cup of tea. He was seated on a wooden bench next to a wobbly tin table with a gaudy cloth spread over it. Just as he was about to sip his sweetened tea, the two boys appeared and gestured to him.

Nandu followed them. They took him through some narrow bylanes till they reached a house with a green door. The door was ajar. All of them entered.

Seated in a small dingy room were a few men his age. Seeing Nandu, they got up from the diwan and came forward to embrace him. 'Welcome, dear brother!'

Nandu was confused. Such a warm welcome from strangers was unexpected.

'Brother, your information was exemplary. It did shake the British government a bit. This is just the beginning of what you have done for us. We remain highly indebted to you,' one of the men said.

Nandu, still in a bit of shock, replied, 'I had vowed to be a part of this movement, and I shall do whatever I can in my limited capacity. I did what I thought was right. I seek no praise and glory. This is my duty to my motherland.'

'Well said, well said! Bravo!'

Assured that this was not a trap, Nandu made himself comfortable. A young woman walked in with some teacups on a steel plate. Vimla's image flashed before Nandu's eyes. He remembered their light-hearted conversations while making tea in his room. He reached for a cup.

The men around him started talking animatedly. One of them, who called himself Sartaj, silenced everyone and came to sit closer to Nandu. 'Brother, we know that you are being sent to Calcutta and will be working with a silk trader. Perhaps you will meet the members of the Jugantar group or the Anushilan Samiti. Both are very active in Calcutta. We want you to do something for us.'

He continued after a pause. 'Tomorrow, we will give you some bales of silk that have come from China. They will be wrapped around long wooden cylinders. These cylinders are meant to be hollow, but in your case they won't be. We are smuggling some powder within the cylinders. The powder is essential for making hand grenades. The bales and cylinders together will weigh heavier than usual so you will have to be careful. Ensure they don't touch water or fire, or you will have Diwali on your hands,' he said with a laugh.

He continued, 'At the Howrah station, someone will meet you as a coolie and offer to help with your luggage. You can hand over the bales to him. He will demand an anna to carry them, which will be your cue. Remember, he will ask for nothing but an anna. Give him that and the bales. He will walk in front of you, but he will soon disappear. Easy enough?'

Nandu considered this. Many thoughts cropped up in his head. *How do they know where I am going? Does Vimla know about my destination, too?* He contained his thoughts and said, 'Yes, at this point it does sound easy. I guess the police will not suspect me as I am slated to be in Calcutta for work anyhow. I know a bit about the silk trade myself, and talking about it won't be much of an issue. Where and when will you deliver the bales to me?'

'We will give it to you at the station, just before you board the train. One of us, pretending to be a silk merchant, will meet you and request you to carry the samples. He will give you an address, a fake one, where it needs to be delivered. Now you must go back and collect the sweets that you ordered.'

Bidding goodbye with a hug, they dispersed amidst calls of an 'Azad Bharat'. The two boys brought him back to the shop where his parcel was ready at the counter. Nandu briskly walked back to the house and handed over the sweets to the elder brother, who thanked him and said it was their duty to be of help. 'I do hope you enjoyed your stay with us. You needn't have bought the sweets!' he said.

Both of them vowed to be in touch. But Nandu was already elsewhere. Tomorrow was another day, another destination. He had a responsibility to execute carefully.

CALCUTTA

8

Goodbyes had become a way of life for Nandu. First, he had to leave behind his family, friends and village; then it was Sharmaji and the others in Amritsar, especially Vimla, and the soul-tearing thought of never being able to see her again; and now it was his host family in Delhi. Although Nandu had stayed with them for a short while, he had been happy to be a part of a family again. The familiar sounds from the kitchen, the smell of vegetables cooking and the asafoetida sizzling in oil reminded him of his home and gave him a sense of belonging.

Here he was again, out in the cold, on his own, navigating his way through an alien world. He took leave of everyone, touched the feet of the grandparents, made promises to visit if he returned to Delhi and was back on the road with his trunk.

At the station, a portly man with a gold chain around his thick neck and several rings on his finger approached him. He introduced himself as Lala Dinanath and requested Nandu to carry some goods to Calcutta. He then called a young boy carrying three bales of silk. It was ordinary printed silk in bright red, ochre and blue, not more than twenty metres each. As promised, the bales were heavy. Nandu gingerly balanced his trunk in one hand and the bales in the other. Lala Dinanath pushed a small chit of paper into Nandu's hand. It had the name and address of a shop in New Market. The word 'New Market' filled Nandu with hope. It was the area where Vimla's cousin lived. Maybe he would meet her again, talk to her and rekindle the relationship that had ended so suddenly.

Lala Dinanath said, 'You won't need the address. This is proof, you understand, right?'

Nandu nodded. The train was about to leave.

He found his seat and sat down with a sigh. In his compartment were a married Bengali couple and an old man visiting his son and daughter-in-law. After exchanging pleasantries, they got busy reading a book, dozed off or kept talking among themselves. They did not seem very keen on speaking to Nandu. In any case, Nandu was busy balancing the bales on his lap, mindful of their contents. The journey was long and tedious. After a while, his legs and hands felt numb. Once or twice, his co-travellers asked him to keep the bales down, but he politely declined, explaining that the dirt might stain the material.

Before long, Nandu also dozed off despite his stomach rumbling with hunger. At dawn, the train reached Howrah Station. As soon as Nandu got down, a man in beggar-like clothes came running towards him.

'Babu, I haven't eaten for a day. Give me one anna and I shall take the load from you and walk with you towards your destination,' he said.

Nandu, who was still groggy, took a few minutes to realize who the man was.

The beggar repeated, 'Only one anna, babu. That will buy me some food. Just spare an anna, and I will help you carry the load.'

Nandu handed over the bales and warned the man not to drop them. The man started walking a few steps ahead of Nandu. He called out to the man and gave him the address, saying that he should wait for his payment there. The man kept walking ahead of him and vanished soon. Everything had played out as decided.

Nandu took a deep breath and looked around. He was in Calcutta, a city that he had heard so much about. His history lessons had taught him about Nawab Siraj-ud-Daulah, the East India Company's foray into Bengal and the political unrest during Lord Curzon's rule. Nandu tried to soak in the sights and sounds of the city, delighted to finally be in this historically significant place.

He slowly walked towards his destination, as per instructions from the cantonment: Aung San Traders, a shop selling Chinese and Japanese silk and other luxury items like laces, beads and semi-precious stones. In Chowringhee, he saw the famous Grand Hotel. Indeed, it looked grand with its white pillars and majestic portico. He saw several Britishers going in and out of the hotel. He stopped to look at the glass display of Lyon & Lyon company, that showed off the latest barrel guns. J. Bose Jewellers caught his attention, too. The beautiful necklaces reminded him of Vimla and her slender, swan-like neck. He sighed. A sense of loneliness rose in him like a column of black smoke and enveloped his heart. He felt a dull ache in his chest. He hurriedly rubbed it with his free hand and walked ahead briskly.

It wasn't very difficult to locate the shop in the New Market area, or Hogg Market. Everyone there knew Rangoon Sahib's shop. The owner, Mr Aung San*, was a petite elderly man with a balding head that had just a few strands of hair neatly combed back with oil. He wore a loose shirt and flared pants. He was polite and spoke in a matter-of-fact tone. He showed Nandu to a small room at the back of the shop. It had a bed, a cupboard and a desk. Food, Nandu was told, was easy to find, and that he would soon get used to the Bengali way of eating fish and rice for all meals. 'That's what we people from Rangoon eat, and that is what the people here eat. Today you must rest, eat and look around. This market is a maze, which you must get used to. Tomorrow, I will explain your work. You will need to go to the dock several times to unload the material coming in from Rangoon, besides manning the shop. I will also introduce you to a bunch of people who will help you please your bosses in the cantonment,' Aung San said with a wink.

As soon as he left, Nandu fell flat on the bed. He was mentally and physically exhausted. He was worried whether the bales of silk had reached their destination. If the man was caught, the police could trace him as the bearer of the goods from Delhi. He took deep breaths to calm down. The smell of fried fish, lingering in the air, made him feel worse.

Adjusting to a new place, a new bed and new sounds and smells was not easy, but Nandu was so tired that he drifted off to sleep instantly, dreaming of fleeing while holding Vimla's thin wrist, her bangles tinkling violently. In his dream, both of them were concerned about the sound of her bangles giving them away. Next he knew he was in his village, eating under the mango tree and his mother was putting extra pickle on his plate. Even in his dreams, he yearned for a calmer life. Yet here he was, in a city that didn't speak his language, where no one ate the food he was used to.

Nandu sat up drenched in sweat. He went to the washroom nearby, a common space for all those who worked in the shop, and splashed water on his face, neck and hair and changed his shirt. He was not used to the sticky and humid weather of Calcutta. It was nothing like the heat in Punjab. He decided to step out and see the market, to note the lanes and bylanes, to identify shops as cues that would help him find his way.

Outside, it was brightly lit with freshly fried food being served to customers. Women dressed in gaudy colours were walking around. Perhaps, Nandu wondered, these were the prostitutes who were always mentioned in a hushed manner in his village. Some of them stared at him, some giggled and some used gestures to call him closer. He averted his eyes and slipped into another lane selling shoes and faux leather handbags. Throughout, he secretly wished that he would bump into Vimla. Perhaps she, too, was out like him, shopping with her cousin. But it didn't happen.

He spotted an eatery selling hot rotis and vegetables. His stomach rumbled in response. He realized that he had not eaten anything since the day before, barring the cup of tea that was offered by his employer. He ate hungrily and made a mental note of the eatery's location. Perhaps it would become his haunt till he got used to fish and rice. Feeling a lot more energetic and positive, Nandu stayed out for another hour, until the shops closed for the day.

Nandu decided to post a letter to his parents the following morning. He had not written to them since he was in Delhi. Perhaps he could write to his sister, too, to take care of his boring first evening in Calcutta. A while later, the neatly folded letters were ready. He then snuggled inside his sheet, wondering what life in this city would present him with, what his work would be, but all those thoughts had to wait till he got a call from Charles with instructions.

9

Nandu's work at Aung San's shop was no different than that at Lalaji's. Only, it was on a much larger scale. He was asked to maintain accounts, check the inventory, help with the sales and often attend to the customers. Nandu found himself struggling to adjust, struggling to tackle the bones in the fish, struggling to communicate, struggling to eat curries made with a generous amount of sweetness. He yearned for a life that was familiar.

The biggest difference here was the customers: they were mainly junior officers from the British government, their wives or friends and members of the Anglo-Indian community, who treated Indians as coolies and never bothered to engage in a conversation. The segregation was stark, the workers were considered too lowly to be engaged with. This was very different from where Nandu had worked earlier, where everyone asked about each other's well-being and even shared tales of happiness and woe. Nandu realized that if he wanted to thrive here, he would have to stop trying to make friends.

Aung San didn't make any attempt to introduce Nandu to the revolutionaries. It resulted in mounting pressure from Charles, who was impatient to receive news of their activities in Calcutta—he had information about a big attack and wanted Nandu to establish a link as soon as possible. 'Do whatever it takes. Even if that means sitting on their doorstep all day, do it. We have spent enough money on you. Your family home is getting renovated with whose money, my dear lad? Surely, you don't want them to know what you do for a living.'

Nandu realized that Charles's desperation was pushing him to issue these threats. He tried to reassure Charles, but he knew these were false promises. He wondered if talking to Aung San once more would help. The shop owner had been dodging the topic on the pretext of being busy. The consignment coming for him from China, via Rangoon, was more important to him than serving Nandu's white masters. Nandu, meanwhile, couldn't risk his parents, or anyone else in the village, learning what he did for a living. He knew that Charles was quite capable of spreading the news if it suited him.

Nandu had never believed in any deity, but he did pray occasionally and attended rituals when forced to do so by his mother. The thought of his mother caused his heart to ache. Tears flowed from his eyes. He blinked hard to contain them, hoping that no one had seen him in that weak moment—standing in an alien city, lost, nostalgic, confused and vulnerable. He wished he had his father's strong shoulder to lean on, or his mother's soft lap in which to hide his face.

There was no coming back from what he had signed up for. He prayed for a miracle to his mother's Rabba, hoping that his wish would be heard.

Nandu didn't have to wait long. Whether it was God's doing or sheer good luck, an unexpected opportunity came his way. His friend Ajit had once called him manipulative. Maybe he was. He had to do what was needed to survive.

The new consignment of silk and laces had reached the docks. Nandu was assigned to get the clearance and bring it to the shop after counting each box and jute-wrapped packet, ensuring nothing got damaged because of the rain or the mud. Since he was very new to the system, he asked Asit, a junior clerk, to accompany him.

Asit, a quiet man in his late twenties, was short, dark-complexioned and so thin that his clothes seemed to hang on his body. He wore spectacles that he kept pushing up the bridge of his nose every few seconds. He hardly spoke to anyone in the shop and disappeared with his small tin lunchbox in the afternoon. No one knew where he went, and no one asked.

It was Nandu's first time in a tram car. He was as excited as a little child when the tram moved around the city like a coiled snake. He watched the man in uniform, who collected the money and tugged at a rope to keep people away, in awe. Nandu wished his brothers, Dhannu and Ballu, were with him. They would have clapped their hands in glee.

Nandu sat next to Asit. Asit was not much of a talker, but Nandu managed to find out that he lived with his widowed mother, that his two sisters were married and lived in distant villages and that he had lost his father to an illness when he was only five years old. He had had a hard life, living mainly on alms given by relatives and the little his mother earned doing some stitching work and odd jobs in houses during marriages or other functions.

Asit had started working in an eatery when he was fourteen. He hadn't been able to study much; he could just about read and sign his name. Nandu shared his own story with Asit, describing his village, the vast mustard fields and how lovely they looked in full bloom, his family and their mango and lime trees.

Asit barely spoke when Nandu was talking, but at the end he said, 'Maybe, one day, I will get the chance to see a field filled with yellow flowers. I would love that.'

As silence descended over the pair, Nandu decided to look out of the window and watch the city go by. He was awestruck by the huge houses, the rows of shops selling all the latest wares and a few cars. He was intrigued about how they ran. Asit guessed his question and said, 'They run on fuel.'

By now, the tram was close to the dockyard. When they alighted, Nandu started making a mental note of the alleys and bylanes. He wanted to be able to navigate his way around in case he was sent alone the next time.

It was dark by the time they reached the dock. Nandu noticed how deserted and eerie-looking the dock was, with just some gas lamp posts here and there. A man, who seemed to be waiting for them, led them to the godown and showed them the bundles and boxes. Asit went to get a tonga to load the goods. Nandu signed the challan and started counting the bundles—twenty-one in total. Some of them looked smaller than the others. *Maybe those are the laces and other accessories the memsahibs need for their dresses.*

Asit came with a tonga. After some haggling, the loading began. Asit insisted that Nandu familiarize himself with the surroundings while he took care of the loading. Nandu gladly stepped out of the damp and claustrophobic godown to breathe in the fresh breeze. He was looking at the sea for the first time. Deep in his being, he felt a tug, as if the sea was beckoning.

Asit came to him, panting, a while later. 'It is done. Let's leave. It is already dark, and I need to walk back home. The roads are not safe anymore, and my mother gets worried. And God forbid if it rains! The bales should be in our shop's godown before that happens. Rangoon Sahib won't be pleased if they get wet.'

Nandu sensed something odd. Asit seemed impatient. The man who was very quiet earlier was now rambling about roads, his mother and rain. Something was not right. Nandu couldn't figure out what had changed in a few minutes. Just as he was about to sit in the tonga, he decided to trust his instinct and count the bundles once more.

This agitated Asit. 'Why, dada, you don't trust my counting? I don't see the sense behind this. You have a readymade bed at the back of the shop. You won't understand what this delay means to me. I don't think it is necessary. We can always count in the shop tomorrow. You have been here for barely a month; I have been working here for much longer. I am surprised that you are doubting me,' he said, his pitch rising gradually.

Nandu was sure that something was wrong. He refused to give in to Asit. Nandu ordered the tonga driver to stop and asked the coolie to unload the bales, promising to pay an anna more for the extra work.

Asit was in a rage. His protests grew louder, but Nandu ignored him. He slowly counted the bundles. There were twenty. One was missing.

Nandu turned to his companion. Asit insisted that there had been twenty bundles to begin with, that Nandu had made a mistake. He even threatened to report Nandu to the boss on grounds of harassment.

Nandu had controlled his temper all this while, but now he dragged Asit and pinned him against a wall. In a steely voice, he said, 'Asit Babu, never teach me how to count or point out my mistakes; I seldom make any. I suggest you come out with the truth, or I will leave you pinned against this wall. You will be discovered tomorrow morning, and I will pretend that I know nothing about your sorrow, as everyone in the shop knows that you like staying aloof and alone. I will tell them that you decided to stay back for a while and that I left with the goods, hoping that some time alone would make you feel better. How does that sound?'

Asit collapsed and broke down. His pupils were dilated with fear and he started mumbling. In between sobs, he admitted that he worked for the Swadhinata Sangramis, the fighters for independent Bharat. He explained to Nandu how the work boosted his self-esteem and confidence. For him, the work he did for his motherland was like freeing his own mother from all the insults and hardships she had to face throughout her life—begging for work, not having adequate money, raising three kids alone. Asit was inconsolable.

Nandu looked at him calmly and asked where the missing bundle was and what it contained.

Scared, Asit said, 'It has ammunition, gunpowder and a few pistols that are coming from Rangoon. The twenty-first bundle is not listed in the consignment. No one will notice that it is missing.'

He also said that the Swadhinata Sangramis would pick up the bundle, which was hidden under old sacks and hay, in an hour. They used Aung San's boats to bring the smuggled goods in from Rangoon which carried the consignments of silk and other dress materials for his shop. Since Asit was always in charge of the loading and unloading, he was trusted to carry out the work. He feared that if this secret was divulged, the revolutionaries would kill him. After all, death was the only penalty for traitors.

Nandu realized that this was the moment he had been waiting for. He signalled the tonga driver to wait and, in a soft voice, said, 'Asit Babu, let us sit on the steps there. I'll tell you a story.'

Nandu began, 'I have been feeling empty since coming to Calcutta. My main purpose behind coming here was to become actively involved in the revolution. Today, I think I finally see the light at the end of the tunnel. Your secret is safe with me. Our goal is the same, to free our motherland. Please take me to your next meeting. I am very resourceful and may be able to help the cause, like I did in Amritsar. Now, we both have secrets that we must keep to ourselves. Come, my brother, let us return to the shop.'

A tearful Asit hugged Nandu and promised to take him along for a meeting the following Tuesday. 'We have all heard about Amritsar and would be very honoured to welcome the mastermind of such a plot, dada. Your brother is with you in this mission,' he said and thumped his chest.

Once again, they hugged each other and said 'Vande Mataram' in low voices before heading back. Nandu felt a twitch. He hadn't told Asit the whole truth: the real reason he was sent to Calcutta. But Nandu could not trust anyone; he needed to be very cautious. He was maintaining a delicate balance in his life. Even a small mistake could spell disaster.

A the tonga moved through the city and night descended, the calm of the sea reflected in Nandu's mind. He felt as if he was finally getting somewhere.

10

Asit thought of himself as insignificant, but he was a diligent worker who stayed true to his work and words.

On Tuesday morning, he entered the shop while Nandu was jotting down the number of silk bales and segregating the printed ones from the plain-coloured ones. Pretending to examine the cloth with him, Asit whispered, 'Dada, remember, today is Tuesday. I have already spoken to them. They are eager to meet you. I will come to your room at 6.30 p.m. If anyone asks, we are going for dinner. You follow me but stay a couple of steps behind. It is a bit of a walk through a maze, so don't lose sight.'

Nandu nodded and took a deep breath. He could feel his pulse at the nape of his neck. Excitement always impacted his hunger; he barely ate any lunch. He kept looking at the big wall clock as its hands slowly inched from morning to afternoon and finally the evening. Although the shop was open till 8 p.m., Nandu excused himself early. Aung San dismissed him with a wave, busy checking his profit and loss statements. There were not many customers at that time, so he didn't mind if some of the workers wanted to leave early.

Nandu went to his room, changed into his usual clothes and waited for Asit. Right on time, there was a mild knock.

'Dada, please follow me. Remember to walk a few steps behind. Be casual, as if you are out for a stroll.'

The walk seemed endless. Asit purposely took a circuitous route. Some of the lanes were poorly lit, some were silent apart from a few stray dogs, some had stalls with people selling vegetables or frying pakoras. Calcutta seemed to have a different aroma, different from any other city. Was it the smell of mustard oil, fish or just the damp soil? Nandu couldn't be sure. He didn't know if he would be able to get to the meeting place on his own. Maybe he would after a few more visits.

That day, he wasn't concentrating much on the route. His objective was to not lose sight of Asit. The humidity was already making him sweat; his kurta was clinging to his broad shoulders.

Finally, in Beniapara Lane, they reached a dead end where a lone house stood. The house, which had probably been grand at one point, looked rather dilapidated. There were pieces of broken statutes near the entrance. The arch in front of the door must have had animals and deities carved into it, but age and neglect had made them indistinguishable.

Asit knocked thrice on the wooden door. Someone from inside enquired who it was, and he said his name. There was a loud clang as the door was unlocked. Despite its weather-beaten appearance, it seemed well-secured. They were greeted by a boy who was no more than fourteen years old. The boy pointed towards the staircase and said in a solemn voice, 'Go upstairs.' Asit ushered Nandu to follow him.

There were three rooms upstairs, all of which were occupied. The people in the first two rooms looked at Asit, smiled in recognition and carried on with their work.

They entered the last room, where three men, probably in their late thirties or early forties, sat. Introductions were made and greetings were exchanged. They mainly spoke in Bengali, which was hard to follow for Nandu. One of the men noticed Nandu's blank stare and started translating in Hindi. This gentleman was Atindranath Ray*, but he preferred to be addressed as Atindra.

Nandu learned that these men were professionals—lawyers, teachers and even a doctor—who assembled almost every evening. If someone didn't arrive, the others understood that they were under vigilance. At Atindra's behest, Asit gave Nandu a tour of the house.

Nandu was told that the other two rooms had junior volunteers writing fiery speeches and pamphlets, organizing rallies and occasionally working on some 'big project of elimination', where they plotted to kill some high-ranking British official. On the ground floor, at the back of the house, two rooms were kept for assembling guns and making hand grenades and other ammunition. To an outsider, these rooms looked like kitchens and storehouses for wood.

Two women joined them later. One was Atindra's wife, Surama, and the other was a local teacher, Anila. They brought in some tea and biscuits. Nandu wished to ask them about Vimla—he was sure that she must have already joined the group—but he knew it would be inappropriate to do so on the very first day. Somewhere, the hope of seeing her again was reignited in his mind.

All of them were eager to hear what their counterparts were doing in other parts of the country. Nandu was asked about his role in the Amritsar shootout, and he filled them in as much as he could.

After almost an hour, Atindra asked Nandu how he could be of help to them. It was Nandu's turn to elaborate on his contribution. 'I came here with Asit, and I am most grateful to him for that. I understand that you get consignments from China via Rangoon, mainly ammunition. With increasing vigilance, I feel it will become difficult for one of you to get the bundle from the dock and bring it here. It can get dangerous and if you get caught, the effort and money are wasted. I suggest that we take the bundle to the shop and keep it hidden under my bed in my room, which is just behind the shop. No one comes there, and it is locked when I am in the shop. I hardly leave the vicinity, except for meals. I can bring the bundle to any shop in Hogg Market or you can pick it up from my room. Does that sound good? This is what I can think of, apart from translating your English pamphlets to Hindi and Gurmukhi to attract more people. Do you think this might help?'

Atindra was very happy. Reaching the dock in time to retrieve the bundles before they were discovered and then bringing them to the house while evading notice was a difficult task. They had nearly been arrested once. Nandu was made responsible for hiding and handing over the parcel to them.

Atindra asked him, 'Do you know Bowbazar Street? Have you been there? I am sure you have heard about the tabloid *Jugantar*. 93/A in Bowbazar is where the arms are assembled and hand grenades are made. Perhaps you can drop the parcel there.'

Nandu had never been there. Asit quickly jumped in, 'I know the place, dada. Rangoon Sahib has sent me a couple of times to pick up merchandise. I will go with Nandlal.'

Atindra was satisfied.

The other gentleman, Shankar, who was a teacher, asked Nandu an unexpected question. 'Brother, how big is your room? Can you describe it to us?'

Nandu was taken aback. He mumbled, 'Ah, well ... it is not very big. Calling it a room might be a bit of an exaggeration. It is a part of the shop, perhaps meant to be its second godown. It has a bed, a small wooden cupboard and just enough space to keep my small trunk and some necessities like a water jug and a tumbler. There are no windows, so it can be a bit claustrophobic, but I usually keep the door ajar for some fresh air. I have nothing worth stealing anyway. Who wants to take some old clothes? The toilet is a bit far and is common. The room has not been maintained well and there are damp patches on the wall. The floor is also broken at places. To be honest, it is nothing great.'

Shankar thumped the table. 'This is what I wanted to know. No window, locked door, nobody comes, old and dilapidated, doesn't attract any attention. Now, you need to do us a favour. Can you?'

Nandu waited for him to elaborate.

Shankar started narrating. 'You saw the boy who opened the door. That is Manmatho. He has come from Dhaka with his brother, Samonto. Both of them are in their teens. They have lost their parents, and their sole purpose is to serve the country. They are very committed to this cause. We need to keep them safe for two to three days, till we send them to Kashi, where we have some work for them. Can you take them with you? They are quiet, will sleep on the floor and eat whatever you give them. Can you do this for us? If you can, it will be a great help. They are an asset to us. We don't want them to be caught.'

Nandu agreed, cautioning them about the state of the room again. The boys were called and introduced to Nandu. They could hardly speak in Hindi, and their Bengali dialect was different from what Nandu had become used to. The situation was explained to them and they were asked to bring their small bundle of clothes. The boys looked at Nandu with apprehension. Nandu assured them that he, too, had two brothers back home and would do everything to keep them safe and comfortable.

As his words were translated to the boys, they smiled for the first time. Something tugged at Nandu's heart. He longed to see his brothers.

Asit walked the three of them back to the shop and then got lost in the crowd. Nandu opened the lock to his room and ushered the two brothers in. He pointed at the floor beside his bed, where they could spread their gamchhas and sleep at night. Nandu went out to have dinner after locking the door from outside and came back with some rice and curry for the boys, which they gobbled hungrily. Nandu asked them to drink from the water jug and, if needed, to tiptoe to the washroom. Both of them declined. Although most of the conversation was done through sign language, Nandu felt quite comfortable. It was as if his two brothers were with him again. His thoughts drifted and he wondered what they were doing back home. Soon, the only noise was the light snoring of three humans who were very different but tied together by the same cause.

Nandu and the boys fell into a routine in just a day. A regime was set in place—tiptoeing to the washroom at 5 a.m. so no one noticed them, a quick bath in cold water and wearing the same clothes because washing and drying would attract attention. Since they were not fond of tea, Nandu got them a packet of puffed rice, locally called muri, with a piece of jaggery in the morning. At night, he got extra rotis packed with curry, rice and lentils. They ate the rice more fondly than the rotis, which Nandu understood. He knew that people in Bengal could eat rice four times a day. Both the brothers mostly kept quiet. They sat on the floor and hummed songs, which had forlorn tunes, or read a book in Bengali that they carried, or lay down and slept, as if very exhausted.

They never objected to being kept locked, which they understood was a necessary precaution, and they did not object to the food given to them. Since Nandu couldn't converse much with them, he wondered what kind of life they had before coming to Calcutta, who their parents were, if they had any other family and why had they chosen a path of sacrifice at such a young age. Everything remained unanswered as language became a barrier.

After three days, almost at midnight, Atindra and Asit came to fetch the two boys. They were to take a train to Kashi early the next morning. Both of them touched Nandu's feet. Overwhelmed, Nandu pulled them into a hug, kept his hand on their hands and told them in Hindi to be safe. How much they understood was anyone's guess, but they both nodded and left. Atindra thanked Nandu. The group disappeared into the shadow of the night.

Nandu stood at the door for some time. He needed a fresh breath of air to rein in his emotions. The two boys had made him realize how much he missed his family and the warmth that came with being among your own people. As tears stung his eyes, a familiar dilemma came back to haunt him. What was important? A life full of adventure or a life of comfort at home?

Rationale took over Nandu's emotions. Was any part of India quiet? The nation was burning, and so was the passion of young revolutionaries plunging into the fire of martyrdom. *When and where will this end? Will I live to see my beloved country free, or will I end up being labelled a traitor by both sides?* There was no apparent answer.

11

It had been almost nine months since Nandu had come to Calcutta. All this time, Charles had not received much from him, apart from scanty information about rallies or protest marches.

Charles was not happy that Nandu was taking so much time to establish contact with the revolutionaries. But when he heard that Nandu had finally succeeded in reaching one of the dens, he was overjoyed. 'Good, good, my boy! I knew if anyone could do it, it would be you. Now I want you to keep your eyes and ears open and give me any news that you get. It doesn't matter how insignificant it is, it may be important for us. I have heard that somewhere in Chittagong a schoolteacher is creating unrest. His name is Surya Sen, and he has an ally called Ganesh. Sen is good with disguise, which is why we are unable to keep track of him, but we know that he is planning something big. Talk to those who come from Dhaka or Chittagong and find out what they are up to. Report immediately,' he instructed Nandu.

Nandu answered in the affirmative, but there was only one thought racing through his mind. *I will give you nothing that will harm my countrymen and their mission.*

All along, he had hoped to meet Vimla. He needed to be worthy of her trust; he wanted her to look up to him as her hero. He was willing to walk miles to make her believe that he had become what she wanted him to be, that he was doing all that he could do for his country. Their bond extended beyond mere love to a desire for a free and independent motherland. Be it at work, while walking down the lonely streets or while sitting in a buzzing bazaar, all Nandu could think of was Vimla. A couple of times he had thought he had seen her and followed her only to realize it was not her, merely someone of similar build and features. It was like chasing a mirage.

He tried to recall their last conversation, so that he could remember the address or some clue that would help him reach her. All that he could recollect was the mention of New Market and a cousin. He felt foolish for not having asked her for more information at the time, perhaps some landmark, building or park. His days turned into nights with a lingering hope and incessant desire to see Vimla again, to sit with her and talk to her. Nursing this raging storm in his heart, Nandu carried on working as if nothing bothered him.

A few days later, when he went with Asit to the house near Beniapara Lane, he asked about Chittagong. The group still knew nothing about him reporting to Charles. Nandu needed to keep it that way to find out more. He told Asit and the others that someone very close to him worked in the Firozpur cantonment and he had heard from his contact that the British had caught a whiff that something was afoot in Chittagong.

Nandu added that any news he received from the cantonment would be passed on to them. The group was thankful and promised that soon Nandu would be a part of their plan. They, too, were awaiting confirmation.

They were in discussion when Shankar stormed in along with Pramatha. He asked for a glass of water and sat down with a thud. 'This is uncalled for. What are our political leaders up to? They want dominion status for our country. It is like selling our motherland to a vile force,' he said.

Atindra came forward and placed a hand on Shankar's shoulder. 'Calm down, my brother. We have heard about the Indian National Congress's Calcutta session. Biplab Da also attended it. We will not agree to dominion status. We want complete freedom, complete azadi. Our struggle will continue,' he said. The room echoed with calls of 'Purna Swaraj'.

Asit, who generally kept quiet, got emotional. 'Dada, Subhas Chandra Bose has called to form the Bengal Volunteer Corps. Major Satya Gupta will take the lead. We should meet them as soon as possible.'

Pramatha now spoke. 'Yes, Dada, let us go and meet him'.

At this, Dilip, one of the younger lads in the group, stood up. He was from a well-known family and was studying medicine. Even though he had joined the group less than a year ago, he was known for devising very intelligent projects. His zeal to work and his well-planned strategies had helped him secure a prime position. 'We are already talking about it. We will tell you more, Asit. We must all join hands to fight this evil force and push them back to where they belong,' he said.

The room was throbbing with energy. Nandu wanted to forget everything and plunge into the independence movement. But, given his limitations, he knew he couldn't. He was on the payroll of the British government and the money he received was sent back home to maintain his family. His role as a British spy would never allow him to dedicate himself fully to the freedom movement, he would be hunted down and his family would be destroyed if anyone ever found out.

Nandu often visited Beniapara Lane, even without Asit. As his job demanded, he sometimes passed on information about protests that were organized and the pamphlets, songs, speeches and plays that were written to condemn the Raj. It was all harmless information that could have been accessed by anyone.

Charles was not happy with these snippets. He wanted more. Nandu, too, was finding it immensely difficult to balance both his roles. Under no circumstance was he willing to risk his new friends and the cause they were fighting for. He tried to find a way out, and after much thought, he came up with a plan and decided to discuss it with the revolutionaries.

At the next meeting, around seven days later, he told them about the impending danger that Sen, the schoolteacher in Chittagong who was of particular interest to Charles, was in. He added that it was imperative to distract the Britishers.

'What is your plan? What do we do?' someone asked.

Nandu outlined his idea. 'The next time a shipment comes for the store, let us get a consignment of spare arms and ammunitions hidden in it. I will pass on information to the police that Surya Sen is bringing the consignment in. We will, of course, ensure the actual boatman escapes by giving the police the wrong time. The police will find some arms, for which they will be lauded by their white masters. Their search for the missing boatman will carry on, diverting their attention from Sen. We will gain at least fifteen to twenty days while the police chase the boatman and Sen executes his plans in Chittagong. Do you think this might work? Asit and I can tell you when the silk consignment is slated to arrive.'

Dilip put his hand on Nandu's shoulder and said, 'Sounds like a good plan, but we need to execute it meticulously. You do what needs to be done at your end, and we will discuss it internally. Hopefully, by your next visit, we will have some information for you.'

One day, Asit said to Nandu, 'Dada, you have been in Calcutta for almost a year now. You confine yourself to work, the shop, the market and Beniapara Lane. Let us go and see the city on Sunday, when the shop is closed.'

Nandu, who had hardly seen Amritsar and Delhi, agreed immediately. He needed to take his mind off the anxiety about the future.

Together, they went to take a dip in the ghats along the Hooghly river, visited the Dakshineswar Kali temple and savoured the food at the local stalls. In the evening, they went to see the Victoria Memorial. The day remained etched in Nandu's memory forever. It was a day when he did not have to think of his job, identity or responsibilities. He only missed his family and Vimla.

A week later, Nandu told Charles about an impending shipment that Sen was probably bringing into Calcutta. He added that this was something he had learnt during casual conversations and that this wasn't confirmed news. Charles was happy, nonetheless. He finally had something concrete to share with his seniors. He instructed Nandu to stay alert and report any more information to him immediately.

Everything moved as planned. Nandu was told that Sen, too, was happy about the diversion. He and his aides had no one trailing them.

Once the details were fine-tuned, Nandu informed Charles about the day the boat was supposed to arrive at the docks. As planned, he gave Charles the wrong time.

On the designated day, Asit and Nandu reached the docks early. After unloading the shipment, they took charge of the bundle that had the ammunition. The boatman was told to escape as soon as he heard the police coming. A horse carriage was kept ready to take him away from the dock. The boatman knew that he had to stay disguised as Sen and disappear into the bylanes.

Asit left after the unloading, while Nandu guarded the bundle. As soon as the police arrived, he handed it over to them and pointed to where the boatman had alighted and disappeared into the night. The police, alert and frantic, went after him.

Exhausted, Nandu decided to walk to Beniapara Lane but purposely avoided the usual route. He was happy at having staged a double game where Charles was satisfied and Sen got time to carry out his plan, which Nandu knew nothing about. On his way back, Nandu entered a post office and sent a telegram to Charles. It had just two words: Work done. Nandu was not in the mood to engage in a conversation or offer detailed descriptions. He felt drained and inadequate. He wondered where this cat-and-mouse game would lead him. As he manoeuvred the lanes, images of his mother wiping her tears, his father placing a hand on his shoulder and his brothers laughing flashed through his mind. His heart ached to see them again. He longed to get away from the cities where he didn't belong, where no one knew him. As the adrenaline ebbed, he found himself thinking of his fate if he got caught. He would be stamped on and marked as a traitor by both sides. Nobody would remember his contribution. Worse, he would be maimed or killed and dumped in a ditch. Nandu doubted his own existence; dark thoughts clouded his mind and left him in low spirits.

Nandu reached the house in Beniapara Lane and hurried upstairs. He knew the revolutionaries were waiting. His throat parched, he asked for a glass of water. As he absently stretched his hand to take the brass tumbler, he was taken aback. The hand that held out the glass was Vimla's. There she was, clad in a simple saree, red bangles on her thin wrists and vermilion in her hair. Their fingers touched briefly, but Nandu jerked his hand away, splashing some water on Vimla.

Vimla softly asked Nandu in Hindi, 'How have you been? Are you okay? We tried to locate you after hearing that you are in Calcutta.'

Before Nandu could answer, Madhav came in from the next room and slapped him hard on the back. 'Brother, we meet again! I told you our paths would cross. Surprised to see Vimla? We got married last month! Her family was putting a lot of pressure on her. After all, she was an unmarried woman staying with her cousin in Calcutta, away from her family in Punjab. They are at peace now that she is with her husband, and we work together as we used to.'

Nandu gulped down some water and mumbled his congratulations. Madhav took him to the next room. 'Meet the women who are an integral part of our group along with Vimla. Here is Rani, who is also known as Pritilata, Sujata, Mahamaya, Supriti, Benoda and Lakkhi. Don't go by how fragile they look. They are more educated than us and as fierce as tigresses. And they are involved in Master Da's plan.' At Nandu's confused expression, he clarified, 'Master Da meaning Surya Sen, as most people know him. We will shake the British Raj in every way possible. Each blow will cost them dearly. We are happy to have you among us, my brother. Tell us how you managed to pull off this chase today. It was so clever!'

Vimla, too, came in and sat down.

While eager eyes looked at Nandu, waiting to listen to his story, he felt drained of all hope, as if the precious memory that he had held so close to his heart, a memory he hadn't shared with anyone, had been stolen from him. He felt empty and hollow; his throat was parched, and he struggled for words.

It took him a few moments and some deep breaths to be able to narrate what had transpired at the dock. Everyone praised him and congratulations floated in from everywhere. But Nandu could hardly comprehend what was being said, he only saw Vimla's large eyes looking at him. Though they did not speak to each other, they communicated through the silence.

Suddenly, Nandu got up and left, mumbling that he had work at the shop. He wanted to escape that room; he couldn't bear to see those large eyes fixed on him.

Vimla followed him. Downstairs, just before Nandu stepped out, she said, 'Wait, don't go away without talking to me. I know you are upset, but what could I do? I was a young, unmarried girl away from home. My aunt didn't want me in her house, and I couldn't live alone. I couldn't have gone back to Amritsar. Madhav was the only person who came to visit me regularly. Even that became a point of gossip for my neighbours and relatives. I didn't know where you were and whether we would meet again. Madhav was my only choice. He is a good friend and as committed to the cause as I am. I had to make a decision. Madhav loves me, and I am now his wife. What happened between us is a thing of the past. What we felt for each other doesn't matter anymore. Please don't speak about it to Madhav.'

Nandu sighed. 'Is this what you fear? That I will talk about our precious moments to Madhav? I am sorry to know that this is what you think of me. If you need assurance, I promise the past will remain in my heart. I will not talk about it, but you cannot erase those evenings from my memory. I am also sorry that I couldn't hold your hand that evening. For months after, I didn't know where to find you. We never thought that evening would end so abruptly. Alas, our lives were meant to take another turn. I wish you all the happiness with Madhav.' Saying this, Nandu rushed out. He didn't want to be there a moment longer. He didn't want to turn and see Vimla trying to control her sobs.

The feeling of loss accompanied Nandu for a long time. Sights, sounds and smells triggered his memories. Everything was a reminder of Vimla. If he closed his eyes, he could imagine her standing in front of him. He lay on his bed for a long time, staring at the roof, his thoughts drifting. He was not in the mood to go out and have dinner. He remembered the red phulkari chaddar that his mother had made for his future bride. His eyes filled with tears. He had pictured Vimla in that shawl!

Nandu didn't know how long he lay staring at the ceiling, but when he looked outside it was pitch dark. He reluctantly got up, drank some water and went back to bed. He hoped the comfort and warmth of the bed would soothe him into a slumber, that it would help him forget what he had lost forever. The city felt unbearable. He wanted to run away to a place where he would never have to meet Vimla or Madhav. He decided to speak to Charles the next day. Slowly, his eyes closed and he drifted into troubled sleep.

RANGOON

12

Everything in Calcutta was getting to Nandu—the food was bland, the sultry weather was too much to bear and the language was difficult to understand. Everything associated with Vimla was losing its charm. All hope had faded into the horizon, leaving Nandu with a dull ache in his chest. It was a daily struggle to believe that Vimla was not his anymore, that she never would be.

Nandu didn't feel like going back to Beniapara Lane. He feared confronting Vimla, and he feared betraying his emotions in front of Madhav and the others. When people came to call on him, he pretended to be unwell. He started spending his time wandering through the streets to avoid the familiar faces who came knocking at his door.

He made several trunk calls to Charles, emphasizing that his work in Calcutta was done, that it was down to a never-ending chase between the British officers and Surya Sen. He explained that most people were undercover and hard to locate. No substantial news was expected for a while, he told Charles, adding that it made perfect sense for him to move to another station to be useful to the cantonment.

Charles was reluctant. Moving an asset was not easy. It required preparation and presented logistical challenges.

Besides, he felt that Nandu could still locate the sleeper cells, befriend the members and find out more about their activities. Charles had heard rumours about innocent-looking young women being educated in Dhaka and Calcutta and being made a part of the movement. When Nandu heard this, he kept quiet. He did not give away the fact that he had already met these women and knew one of them closely. Sometimes, when he felt anger surging in his chest, he thought about extracting revenge by telling Charles about them. Then, the very next moment, he admonished himself for being so selfish. He wished his family or his friend were around him to tend to his wounded soul. There was no one in Calcutta in whom he could confide. He decided to immerse himself in his work, exercise, go on long walks and rest until a new opportunity came up. He wrote several letters to his family, his sister and Ajit, describing his life, although selectively.

The opportunity Nandu was waiting for came soon. During one of his many phone calls to Charles, he was told that the time had come for him to sail abroad. He was to be stationed in Rangoon for a short while, and later head to the Far East, China, the Malay Peninsula, or if he was lucky, Japan.

This news cheered him up. He used a part of his savings to buy new clothes. He also bought shawls for his parents, shirts for his brothers and knick-knacks for his little nephew, packed them with a bundle of money and sent the parcel to his family with someone who was travelling to his village.

Preparations were made for Nandu's travel. He was to board one of the Burma Steam Company's steamers in a few days. The ship would take him to Rangoon through Port Blair. He would enter Burma through Cox's Bazar.

Nandu, who had never sailed in his life, was apprehensive about the journey. After giving it some thought, he decided to make one last visit to Beniapara Lane. Though both Vimla and Madhav were not there when he went, he didn't ask about them, fearing it would draw the others' attention. However, he was disappointed as a part of him had hoped to see Vimla one last time.

At the house, pleasantries were exchanged along with concerns for his health. When he told everyone that he had got a new job in Rangoon, which paid well, their ears perked up. They broke into an animated discussion and excitedly told him that he could connect with the revolutionary cells operating out of Rangoon. Almost 30 per cent of the Burmese population was Bengali, most of whom were from Chittagong, the same place where Master Da was from.

'Chittagong is a name that many British officials will remember for a long time!' said Pradip, one of the young revolutionaries.

Nandu, while leaving Beniapara Lane, reminded himself that whatever happened was for the best. Maybe it was best that he and Vimla couldn't meet. Seeing her might have distracted him. He sighed as he tried to calm his disturbed mind and resumed his brisk walk back to the shop.

While meandering through Calcutta's lanes, probably for the last time, Nandu wondered what life would have been like had he stayed back in Punjab, tending to the farmland and cattle. *Would it have been more peaceful? Would I have found my love and basked in the warmth of my family?* The village seemed so distant now. Its smell and sights were slowly fading from his mind. He could recollect neither the taste of the dal his mother made, nor the tang of the pickles. He had forgotten how the winter breeze felt and the noise of his brothers fighting sounded.

Every sense yearned to dive into memories that were once so dear to him. His thoughts went back to Vimla, to the bridge of her long nose, to the small black dot on her forehead that was now replaced with a red one, the slender nape of her neck where a strand of hair used to curl up, the tinkling of her bangles as she twisted her braid into a knot. Nandu shook his head to break free of the reverie. She was someone's wife. He sighed again and reminded himself that he must let go. He hoped that the impending journey would help him take his mind off all that he desired and craved but would never get.

The designated day arrived. Nandu packed his meagre belongings in his trunk once again and bade farewell to Calcutta, his colleagues and Aung Sang, who gave him twenty rupees as a bonus and promised to meet him when he was in Rangoon next time.

Asit accompanied Nandu to the dock and hugged him. 'Dada, I am losing an elder brother today. The water might take you away, but you will remain in my heart forever.

You are a rare gem. We had nothing in common. We don't even speak the same language. When you first came here, I resented you. With your looks, your ability to speak English and your smartness, you had everything that I didn't. Yet, you gave me the respect that no one has given me. I feel a part of me is going away with you. I don't know whether you will come back to Calcutta or whether we will meet again. But remember that we are joined by the same cause,' he said, his eyes glistening and his voice choking.

Nandu, too, felt a tug in his heart. But he had to do it again, for the fourth time after Firozpur, Amritsar and Delhi—in Calcutta he was leaving behind friends, a brother-in-arms and his love. Nandu hugged Asit tightly. 'I will not forget you. I received so much love and respect from your friends and associates. You introduced me to some of the finest people who are fighting incessantly to make our country a better place to live, who are ready to give up their lives so that our children can breathe freely. I would ask you to visit Rangoon ... I might be able to arrange something once I am there, but I know that you need to take care of your mother. Still, I do hope our paths will cross again. Now, here is something for you. If you refuse, I will be very upset,' Nandu said and pushed the twenty rupees Aung San had given him into Asit's hand.

Asit recoiled. 'No, no, brother. This is your hard-earned money. I cannot take it.' After much persuasion, Asit agreed to accept the money and buy a saree and shawl for his mother. 'This winter, I saw her shivering. I will tell her that her eldest son got her the saree and shawl,' he said and bent to touch Nandu's feet. They embraced once more before Nandu picked up his trunk and walked towards the steamer, the *Baltic*. It was ready to leave. Stepping on to the boardwalk, he turned around to wave at Asit.

A short while later the *Baltic* started its voyage towards the Andaman and Nicobar Islands. Nandu found a bunk bed on the lower deck. The space was already being shared by five men who were sailing to Rangoon in search of greener pastures. Nandu started chatting with them and realized that he was very lucky to be heading to a foreign land with a job in hand. One of the men was called Ramcharan, from Patna in Bihar. Ramcharan spoke fluent Hindi. Like Nandu, Ramcharan had studied till high school and had left behind a large family that included marriageable sisters and young brothers. He planned to work hard and send money home. Nandu understood his sentiments. Eventually, Nandu and Ramcharan went to the upper deck as the small space was becoming claustrophobic.

The journey wasn't smooth for Nandu. He was seasick and threw up everything he tried to eat. Ramcharan never left his side. He put a wet cloth on Nandu's forehead to make him feel better and managed to get cold water for him to drink. He kept telling Nandu, 'This, too, will pass.'

Nandu felt better after the *Baltic* docked in the Andaman and Nicobar Islands. Passengers were allowed to embark and walk on the shore. The captain warned them to not go far as there were man-eaters on the prowl. Whether anyone believed the captain or not, no one ventured too far, fearing the steamer might leave.

On the shore, vendors were selling tea, boiled eggs and biscuits that seemed stale. Nandu, who had barely eaten in two days, and Ramcharan feasted on the food. While they were draining the last drops of the insipid and almost-cold tea, they heard a clang. Two young boys, probably Bengali based on their attire, were being dragged by three policemen. The dried blood on their dusty faces and other injuries suggested they had been beaten up. They were being dragged by the policemen, who had tied their hands and shackled their feet with heavy chains. A thick rope bit into their waists. It was obvious that they were revolutionaries who had been sentenced to Kala Pani, or Cellular Jail, in Port Blair. Kala Pani was infamous for being used by the British to incarcerate political prisoners, revolutionaries and freedom fighters.

The captured boys, who seemed to be in their late teens or early twenties, had probably endured third-degree torture before being brought to the notorious jail. Their future didn't seem to be encouraging.

Ramcharan shook his head and said, 'Bhaiya, what makes them choose this path? This is no less than suicide. Don't they have parents and siblings like us? Don't they want to give them a good life, like we do?'

Nandu was about to defend them, but something made him keep quiet. He had to be careful. He was not very sure whether Ramcharan was an informer or just curious. Nandu nodded and said, 'I don't know, brother. We are mere householders who have left their homes in search of a living. We cannot understand the sentiments and the sacrifice of the revolutionaries and their fight to free our country. We are not here to judge anyone or their actions. Everyone has their purpose and calling.'

'Very right, brother, very right indeed. Every time I talk to you, my respect increases. You must be very well-read. I am just a poor villager who has led a sheltered life. I have not seen much of the world.'

Nandu sighed. 'I, too, have not seen much, which is why I undertook this journey, to see a different country, to earn money and send it home. I am also a simple villager like you.'

As they headed back to the *Baltic*, they felt a surge of energy and apprehension at the idea of living in a new country.

The steamer sailed towards Cox's Bazar in Chittagong, where more Bengalis boarded the steamer. The sand was glistening in the sun and the blue water looked ethereal. Nandu kept looking at it until he was driven away from the upper deck. He and the others scurried back to the lower deck, where the natives were confined.

Although the air in the lower deck was stale, the conversation was animated. It ranged from politics to the freedom movement to hopes and ambitions for a better life. Nandu eagerly participated in all conversations since he could understand a little Bengali. Ramcharan followed him everywhere. At the slightest hint of nausea, he would fetch Nandu salt or cold water. Nandu was grateful for the concern.

Two days later, they were on the Irrawaddy river in Burma. At the first glimpse of a foreign land, Nandu felt that his dreams of seeing the world were turning into reality. He could see the glistening roof of a pagoda, the busy streets near the dock and the familiar hand-pulled rickshaws. He saw men dressed in wraparounds like lungis, tied over their shirts, and women selling food from baskets, their faces smeared with sandalwood paste, which made them look pale.

Once the ship docked, all the passengers went their different ways. Some of them had addresses, while others aimlessly searched for work. Ramcharan had a friend staying in a slum who had promised to find him a job. Nandu and he vowed to meet at 6 p.m. at the same spot in two days. Perhaps, they hoped, they would both have an address to share. Promises were made to keep in touch in this strange land.

Nandu had heard a lot about Rangoon. He knew that several Anglo–Burmese wars had been fought there and that Burma had gradually come under British rule. The teak, ruby and other trades were controlled by the British. Indians came in large numbers to seek employment on the plantations. On Clarke Road and around Dalhousie Park, many Indians would gather to meet other people from their motherland. There were undercurrents of unrest between the migrant population and the Burmese people, but Nandu was yet to witness it.

Nandu decided to cross Strand Road and walk towards Scott Market to find J. David and Co., his place of employment. The instructions given to him by the cantonment were helpful. He passed the famous Strand Hotel, where he saw British men going in and out of the hotel with ladies dressed in fancy frocks and hats. He also crossed the beautiful Shwedagon Pagoda. Nandu was not very religious, but he found himself bowing in reverence before the pagoda. He sent up a prayer to make his stay worthy of the travel and to keep his family safe. The gilded pagoda, against the receding sunlight, looked breathtaking. He decided to visit the pagoda soon and hurried away to meet his employer before the shop closed. It was the beginning of yet another adventure.

13

The sun had set by the time Nandu found J. David and Co. It was on one of the busiest streets frequented by the Britishers and some Europeans. Seeing so many well-dressed people, Nandu felt a little conscious entering the posh showroom. His employer, Mr David, was waiting for him in the back office. He was a plump, red-faced Britisher in his late forties, whose tight necktie gave him a very uncomfortable look, as if he was being throttled. He was sweating profusely despite a ceiling fan and kept mopping his forehead with a large white handkerchief. He didn't seem to be a man of much patience. His voice was gruff, and he made a wheezing sound after finishing each sentence. 'You are late. I thought you had either lost your way or not reached today, although I was informed of your arrival,' he said, measuring up Nandu and the battered trunk that he was holding on to.

'This is not a village. I have high-end customers, so you will have to invest in smart clothes. Don't think that I will give you an advance before you start working. Maybe your original master will,' he added and chuckled.

'No, sir, I don't need an advance. I have some savings. Please give me a couple of days, and I shall find an affordable tailor.'

'Well, you need not do that. I have a tailor who can stitch something for you. We will charge you half the rate, which you can pay back in two months. I shall do that for you, young man. Or one of my men can take you to a tailor's shop meant for people like you. We both have the same purpose. We are here to serve the common goal and are at the service of the British government. Look, man, my aim in life is simple: to remain loyal to my country, to serve it and to make some money in the process. When I have enough money, I will go back to England. I have already sent my wife and daughters home, where they are getting the finest training to become proper ladies. I can't wait to go back and get them married into the gentry. Until then, I will rot in this awful humidity. Of course, there are enough pretty Burmese lasses to take care of all my needs if you throw some coins at them,' he chuckled again, wheezing in between.

Nandu didn't like him, but he reined his emotions in. All he retained were the words 'loyal to my country' and 'go back'. He again wondered whether what he was doing was right and if he would get a chance to atone for his sins. He came back to his senses when David clicked a finger right in front of his nose. 'Man, you reserve your dreams for the night. Now is not the time to get lost in them. Someone will show you your quarters now. You report back at nine in the morning. And remember to take a bath. God knows what infection you may have caught in that deplorable steamer, especially since you travelled with the low-class coolies,' he said, cringing with distaste.

Nandu felt a sense of foreboding. Until now, he had been lucky to find benevolent bosses. Even Charles seemed to be kinder than this man, for whom people not of his race and colour were merely coolies whom he could throw coins at. Resentment and anger rose in Nandu's stomach.

David flicked his finger again. Nandu was ushered away by a thin, gawky Burmese man dressed in a loose half-shirt and grey trousers. He introduced himself as Inzali and said that everyone called him Inza. He ran errands in the store and was a chain smoker. He led Nandu into a bylane opposite the shop and walked up to a house that looked old but was well-maintained. The owner, Kyaw, a man of Sino–Burmese origin, opened the door and introduced himself. Nandu had been designated a small apartment on the third floor.

Nandu was happy to see a tastefully decorated and clean bedroom, with a small kitchen on the side and a bathroom all to himself, which meant he would not have to line up in front of a community toilet anymore. This was a pleasant first.

Kyaw spoke softly. 'We Buddhists like to keep our surroundings clean. Please keep that in mind and don't pile up unconsumed food or rotting vegetables. That will attract rodents and other insects.'

Nandu assured Kyaw that he, too, liked cleanliness and would take special care to keep things in order.

Inza, before leaving, reminded Nandu to be at the store on time. 'Mr David is very angry when people are late. He is master, you obey him. He good, or he very bad. He cut money, punish with hard work. You good man, Indians hardworking and good. I like palata, you know. You want food, you tell me, but not today. Okay, mister, I wish you good sleep. I see you tomorrow,' he said and left.

It took Nandu, who was tired, a while to understand that Inza's 'palata' meant paratha. He was too tired to go hunting for food; he still had some flattened rice and a few pieces of jaggery from Calcutta. That, along with water, would help him get through the night. It did not take him long to doze off on the comfortable bed.

The next morning, he picked out the best white starched shirt he had. The effort drew an appreciative glance from Mr David, whom Nandu politely wished a good morning. Inza was once again summoned to brief Nandu.

The job was the same as it was in Calcutta: keeping a record of sales, inventory, purchases, daily earnings and spending. He also had to keep track of the stock and create a replenishment request, which was forwarded to the purchase officer. The shop itself was not only stocked with the most expensive brocade, silk and cotton but also had a tailoring team that stitched suits and ladies' dresses.

Inza added his two cents, 'Not a button here and there. You count thread and needles, too. Mr David very strict, very angry. He does not like thieves; he punishes thieves.'

At David's behest, Inza took Nandu to a cheap tailoring shop to get two shirts stitched. Nandu's frame was too tall to fit into one of the ready-made shirts. A twinge of guilt clouded his mind. Here he was, getting new and fancy clothes for himself but not sending money home. However, he quickly dismissed the thought. He was doing what was needed to keep his job.

Inza introduced Nandu to Burmese brunch: banana fritters, a rice cake called mont and a thick broth called mohinga, which consisted of noodles, fish and boiled vegetables. It was healthy and tasty, but Nandu couldn't bring himself to eat the fish, which Inza happily took from him. Mohinga, minus the fish, became Nandu's staple for the remainder of his stay in Rangoon.

As both of them walked back to the shop, munching on the sticky and sweet banana fritters, Inza chattered endlessly. Nandu learned that, just before his arrival, there had been a riot between the Indian and Burmese workers. Hundreds were killed and thousands injured.

'Twenty-sixth May. Very, very bad day. Killing all over, shops shut, roads no people. Inza was scared that no food for three days, did not go out. Indian people are hardworking, cheap and take jobs away. But you good. I like you, I like palata, I like to eat palata with you. I feed you.' Through his broken English, Inza managed to explain to Nandu that there was a lot of underlying tension in the city. Nandu made a mental note to navigate the city carefully, without drawing much attention. He knew he had to be cautious and mindful of his activities.

Back at the shop, David handed over a chit to Nandu. It had instructions for Nandu to report to a café in the evening to meet a senior officer called Malcolm Henderson*.

Henderson would explain his work to him, the real reason he was in Burma. Nandu reached the café a little before

5 p.m. Henderson was already there, having a cup of tea. An empty cup on the table told Nandu that Henderson had probably met someone before him.

Henderson was a little over forty years old, blue-eyed, balding near the temples, and sported a bushy hay-coloured moustache that made it difficult to tell whether he was smiling or not. The muscles bulging under his cotton shirt showed that he exercised regularly. He looked kind but Nandu sensed that he could be ruthless if needed.

He asked Nandu to sit, ordered a cup of tea and gestured for the empty cup to be taken away. He clearly commanded respect.

Henderson cleared his voice and spoke, 'No need to introduce yourself. I know all about you and your commendable work in Amritsar and Calcutta. You are documented in a file that is now in my possession. I am your new boss. You will report directly to me. You don't need to contact Officer Charles anymore. As it is, long-distance calls are expensive, and it is not safe to narrate entire reports over a call. Also, the work here is outside his jurisdiction, and you are not in India. Can you type? If you can't, then you need to learn. You can come to my office for that. I expect a typed report every week. Contact me directly whenever you feel the need, or whenever there is an emergency. You need to study the place and its people and familiarize yourself with the culture. You need to gain the confidence of the immigrants, mainly the Bengali men from Chittagong who come here to work but are notorious for triggering riots and helping their revolutionary friends back home.'

He took a pause and leaned forward. 'There is lots to be done and time is limited. Things are getting heated up on all fronts, even in Europe. Don't look so lost. You should probably start by reading a book about Burmese culture and history. The locals like to hear from foreigners about their culture and religion. If needed, you might be sent to the Arakan hills, which are infested with revolutionaries. The Shan state is also known for harbouring them. But you needn't worry. You will always have a local to help you navigate,' Henderson finished.

Nandu had not got a chance to talk so far. He had just been receiving directions on what needed to be done and when. Clearly, Henderson was not someone he could befriend. With him, the line between master and slave was obvious. Nandu left the café with a heavy heart. He realized that he could not balance himself on two boats for long. He had to let go of one. But which one? That was the intriguing question. It was time to contemplate.

14

Nandu spent the next few days working in the shop, familiarizing himself with the lanes and bylanes, settling into the house and getting used to the food, all of which Inza helped him with. Nandu also met Ramcharan and, while sipping tea together, they spoke about their work and accommodations.

Ramcharan had got a job as the caretaker and accountant in a small hotel that provided lodging to the Bengalis who arrived in Rangoon. Calling it a hotel was an exaggeration. It was more of a boarding house for bachelors who came to the city in search of livelihoods. Ramcharan told Nandu that sometimes three to four people shared one room. He added, 'I am the caretaker, but I do everything. From procuring groceries and cigarettes to serving tea or food in the rooms to keeping a daily account of expenses, check-in and check-out, I do it all.'

Then, lowering his voice, he added, 'Brother, I think these people are revolutionaries who have escaped from India. I have heard them talk when I serve the tea. It can put my life at risk, isn't it? What if there is a police raid or something like that? Should I look for another job?'

This conversation interested Nandu. He could probably meet the people he was expected to and file his weekly reports. He assured Ramcharan that he need not change jobs immediately. 'Maybe I should visit you someday and talk to these people. Unless I see for myself, I cannot comment. Until then, I will try to look for a job for you in my shop or in the area nearby,' he told Ramcharan.

The last sentence worked like magic. Ramcharan took the bait. He promised to take Nandu to the boarding house the following Sunday.

Nandu thought of Madhav and Vimla again. He asked Ramcharan, 'Are these only bachelors, or do they bring their wives as well?'

'No, dada. No women allowed. They have come like you and me, looking for jobs. Some of them, however, seem to be in hiding and rarely go out.'

In the week that followed, Nandu tried his hand at the typewriter. It took him a couple of days to type with all his fingers. Even so, typing out one line seemed to take him hours. Henderson, however, remained insistent on typed reports, no matter how much Nandu assured him that his handwriting would be legible. Luckily, there was not much to report in the first few weeks. Nandu used this time to perfect the art of typing.

He submitted his first report after visiting the boarding house. He typed a detailed account of what he had seen, which pleased Henderson. Ramcharan's hunch was correct. There were revolutionaries hiding there, which became evident from the snippets of conversations Nandu and Ramcharan heard while standing in the reception area. Nandu reported this to Henderson, but since there was no evidence yet to support the claim, no action was taken. Henderson was excited, but he held off on taking action and decided to wait for further inputs from Nandu.

Nothing noticeable happened in the first month. Nandu was busy at the shop and mastering new skills. But then, on one of his visits to the boarding house, he noticed a flurry of excitement. The news was that Surya Sen, whom Nandu had come to know as Master Da, had tried to loot an armoury in Chittagong but failed to take away any ammunition. A hunt had been launched for Master Da and his team and, as a result, twelve revolutionaries had been killed in the city of Jalalabad in India. Master Da, known for his disguises, had gone underground. It was suspected that he had escaped to Rangoon to avoid arrest.

Once the news reached the British officers in Burma, Nandu was put on red alert and directed to spend less time at David's store. He started visiting cafés and restaurants frequented by the Bengalis. It was in one such obscure café, while Nandu was sipping his third cup of tea in the evening, that someone slapped him on the back, causing him to spill some tea, and said in a loud voice, 'Brother! So wonderful to see you in this foreign land. It is my ... rather, it is our good fortune.'

Nandu turned around to see Pradip and Pramatha from Beniapara Lane grinning at him. The men embraced, happy to see each other. Hours went by as the trio chatted about the political condition in Bengal, Master Da's escape and how his work had rattled the British empire, and how the women's cell had been trained and was about to execute an equally dangerous operation. Both Pradip and Pramatha were staying in the same boarding house where Ramcharan worked and Nandu had visited earlier. He was invited to be a part of a discussion the next evening. As they said goodbye, Nandu mustered the courage to ask them about Madhav, carefully avoiding Vimla's name.

Madhav and Vimla, Nandu was told, had gone back to Punjab and were operating from Lahore, where they were both teaching in a small school. Vimla was training women revolutionaries to speak in English and Urdu, mainly those who spoke other languages. Nandu thanked them for the information and walked back to his room. The chances of meeting Vimla in this lifetime were getting slimmer. He would have to spend his life with just her image and the sweet memories of Amritsar. He wanted to hold on to them dearly, lest they also fade with time.

The next day onwards, he started frequenting the boarding house more and attended more social gatherings. Nandu had to explain his connection with the revolutionaries to Ramcharan, who was visibly hurt and upset, but he gradually understood the gravity of the situation.

Ramcharan, too, started attending the meetings and listening to everyone with keen interest. Nandu became his mentor. He would often ask Nandu about the plight of his country and his fellow countrymen, and the imprisonment, torture and killing of political leaders by British officials. He realized that he could fight for his country's independence even if he was living away from it. He began helping Nandu with the Hindi translation of the pamphlets and distributing them among those who had come from Bihar.

Nandu, meanwhile, gave Henderson harmless pamphlets calling for the boycott of foreign goods, or details about a gathering that would not fetch an enthusiastic crowd. Such trivial information kept Henderson happy.

Nandu continued with the translation work and helped to print the pamphlets. Sometimes, in the evening, he typed a letter or two in English from Henderson's office, which was posted to revolutionaries who were helping from other foreign countries. He also initiated a rumour that Master Da was planning to come to Rangoon in a dinghy. This was done to give Master Da time to plan his next move, something like what had been done in Calcutta.

One day, Nandu fell ill. He had diarrhoea and couldn't stop vomiting. The doctor told him that it was an acute case of food poisoning, possibly from eating ngapi, fermented fish and shrimp. Nandu couldn't keep even a morsel of food down for two days and could barely drag himself to the toilet. He was shifted to a local hospital and put on a saline drip. For four days, Nandu lay listless and drained of all energy. His eyes were sunken, he was sweating profusely, and the fever had made his skin flaky and dry. He looked like a ghost.

Inza came to see how he was doing. He informed Ramcharan, too, who then visited Nandu twice with fruits and a soup that he had made. Nandu was grateful for the visits. Pradip and Pramatha, too, asked about his health but were unable to come as they were in hiding. Nandu's doctor, who later diagnosed his ailment as cholera, was surprised that he had survived such a bad bout. The illness had left him very weak. He would lie in his bed most of the time, wondering if he would regain his strength or ever see his family again. As time passed, Nandu was convinced that he would die in an alien land.

Two months later, he started moving about again, but his digestive system was impaired. He ate sparsely and survived on boiled food. Henderson was alarmed and decided to talk to the headquarters about shifting him to another country. He knew that Nandu could not be stationed in the Arakan hills or the Shan state, given his fragile condition.

Nandu waited for the verdict. He wished to be sent back to Punjab, but the officials had other plans for him. It was as if the universe had conspired to ensure he would travel to strange lands. His dream of a life of adventure was coming true but at the cost of his health.

SHANGHAI

15

Nandu sat on a beach for a long time, staring blankly at the sea. His world had become like the waves—one incident after the other, one place after the other, one person after the other. He had drifted along, powerless against the tide.

At times, he felt that it was all aimless, without a goal or plan. What was he trying to do? See the world? Escape from a boring, mundane life? Do good for his countrymen? What was it that kept inspiring him to soak into different cultures and lifestyles, reinventing himself for every new beginning?

Several of his friends from the boarding house had planned a picnic despite their meagre incomes. They knew that Nandu was going away. They all agreed that a change of location would be beneficial for his health.

Nandu, however, was running away from all the attention. As he waited for the next chapter of his life to unfold, all he desired was solitude.

When he got back to his room, he found a note telling him to collect his ticket and letter for the journey. This time, the destination was China.

The next day, Nandu was at Henderson's office.

The Britisher offered Nandu a chair. Nandu, mentally and physically exhausted, sat down and accepted the tea that was placed before him for the first time in this office.

Henderson leaned forward, cleared his throat and spoke. 'We are changing our tactics with you, Mr Lal.'

Nandu wanted to correct him. He was Mr Kapur, not Mr Lal. But he refrained. He wanted to hear about the 'tactics'.

Henderson continued. 'Your personality and looks are unlike those of any commoner. Just look at you! Your Grecian features, broad build, the sway in your walk and the way you present yourself are very rare in natives. It is impressive. People simply fall in love with you, be it men or women. We haven't missed that. I wonder how you are still single!' Henderson chuckled and winked before adding, 'We will not send you as a coolie or manager anymore. We will invest in you and make you a sahib like us. A brown sahib!'

Nandu listened intently as Henderson continued. 'I was told that you spent endless hours learning and mastering the silk trade. That will not go to waste. You will now be a trader. Yes, you heard it right. You will enter China as a silk trader, a successful man who is there to sell his wares. There is no information the coolie class can give us anymore. Do you natives think that by removing us from your country, you will gain independence? Humph! You are mistaken, my dear fellow, you are mistaken. We will be replaced by the rich ones in your country; the ones buying you the toys—the pistols and the bombs—will be your new masters. The brown sahibs will make you dance to their tunes. And mind it, they will be tasting power for the first time. They will be as bloodthirsty as man-eaters who eat human flesh for the first time. They will tear you and your countrymen apart.'

Nandu felt like retching. He was in no mood to engage in a conversation about raw flesh, blood or man-eaters. Henderson, however, was relishing the fact that he had a captive audience in front of him, someone who could not get up without his permission. He was enjoying rubbing salt in Nandu's and his countrymen's wounds and trying to gauge how crestfallen Nandu would be after this conversation. Little did he realize that Nandu and all the freedom fighters had nothing but their lives to lose. The prize they were after was the independence of their motherland.

Henderson continued, 'So, now you are going to have a lavish lifestyle, enjoy our wealth and pretend to be a part of the gentry, isn't it? Let me tell you a bit about Shanghai. The city is divided into two parts. One is for us, the Westerners, and the other is for the locals. The Americans and the British control the trade. Shanghai has the busiest port and is responsible for both import and export for the entire country. After the Russian Revolution of 1917, many Russians came and settled down in the city. The western part is thriving with business and modern amenities. There are tramcars, electricity and modern cars in every part of Shanghai. You will open an account with the Bank of China, visit the Shanghai Club, mix with people of our kind and the wealthy Chinese merchants, and find out about their plans concerning the British Empire and Japan. We have information that the Japanese are strengthening their fleet. Maybe the whole world will be embroiled in an endless war. Who knows who will emerge as the winner.'

The last few sentences were tinged with regret. The prospect of an impending war seemed to have unnerved Henderson. Perhaps he, too, was worried about his family. While Nandu had never engaged in personal conversations or tried to find out more about Henderson's background, every detail about him was recorded in a dossier. The officers he reported to simply had to give it a quick read and they would know everything about him. Nandu operated in mysterious ways, but there was no mystery around him, so to speak. Back in Firozpur, he had been taught to listen and never to divulge. Ah! Firozpur. The word felt as sweet as honey on his tongue. He pined for his village, his parents, the mustard fields, the village temple and the festivals. It all seemed so distant.

Henderson had not finished giving instructions. He rattled off information about the flight, the airport, lodging, collecting the money and the bales of silk that would be sent to Shanghai before Nandu reached, and everything else that he needed to know about his work. Lastly, he added that Nandu would have to collect some money from the orderly and buy good clothes, shoes and bags. In less than ten days, he was to board his first British Overseas Airways Corporation flight to Shanghai's Lunghwa Airport. Someone at the store he worked at would help him with the last-minute preparations.

After every detail was memorized and understood, Nandu left Henderson's office.

Nandu's last few days in Rangoon went by in a daze. He could barely think or feel much. The same questions kept running through his head: *Where am I? What do I want? What am I missing in my life?* He started thinking about his life in a chronological order, event after event, but a short while later his mind went blank, and he was left staring at the walls.

He wondered if his illness and medication were playing tricks on his mind. There was complete silence in his small apartment, but he could not think. A thick mist seemed to hang in the air, blocking all rational thoughts and reasoning. All Nandu could sense was the putrid smell of fish sauce, which slowly seemed to envelop his body, mind and soul.

He had to escape; he had to fight this stupor and reignite his passion and focus. He spoke to himself: 'Nandu, you left your home, your loved ones, your comfort, the familiar smells and sounds of the village to see the world. You wanted to help your countrymen; it was your sole purpose in life. It was never Vimla; it was never the estrangement or momentary happiness she gave you. She is in the past, in your memories. And memories don't make you who you are, your actions do. You must act now.'

He battled with himself, every day and every evening, while packing his belongings, bidding goodbye to his friends or trying out a new jacket. The chatter in his head wouldn't stop. Then, one day, he stopped fighting it. Almost immediately, the thoughts evaporated, leaving behind a comfortable silence and the zeal to work harder and excel.

Going to Shanghai was like a dream coming true. It was bringing with it Nandu's first flight, first jacket, first pair of shoes, ties and a duffle bag. He couldn't believe what he saw in the mirror when he tried on his new clothes. Seeing his transformation, he wished his parents had been there to admire him. He knew his brothers would have gone berserk. *What would Vimla have said?* She would probably have teased him, called him an angrez, a sahib. His lips involuntarily broke into a smile.

Nandu was also taken to a photo studio, another first for him. He stood stiffly and couldn't smile even when cajoled. He requested a second copy to send to his parents. They would be happy to see him smartly dressed, looking like a real merchant, like a part of the gentry.

The designated day came, bringing with it another set of goodbyes. It was routine for Nandu. He picked up his bag and headed to the airport, a bit apprehensive about the giant plane that was stuffing people in its belly. He hoped this journey would not be as nightmarish as his first sailing experience. Nandu was curious to know how the plane flew with all its weight. The closer he got to it, the bigger it seemed. As he stared at the plane, its windows and the giant fan in front, Nandu felt a sense of awe, mixed with fear and apprehension. A pretty and well-dressed woman greeted him with a smile, but he didn't know how to respond. He simply nodded.

And then, all of a sudden, he smiled as he wondered what Ajit would have done. When one of the women helped him buckle a belt around his stomach, he felt ticklish. He thanked the universe for allowing him to experience these wonders. With a sigh, he leaned his head back on the soft seat.

16

Nandu enjoyed his first flight. He liked looking at the clouds all around him and the ground from up above, and made a mental note of what he saw to narrate to his family when he met them next. The thought of meeting them someday filled him with untold happiness, but at the same time something churned inside his chest, a premonition, perhaps.

Ching Seng, the man deputed by the British intelligentsia was at the airport to receive Nandu. He was a short Chinese man in his late forties, with a small protruding stomach. He wore a fancy printed shirt and leather shoes, and his thick coarse hair was brushed back and held together with some form of pomade. His handshake was firm and revealed a strength of character, as did his deep voice. He squinted as he took off his horn-rimmed dark glasses, trying to assess Nandu.

Nandu took an instant liking to him. He seemed to know the ways of the world, yet he seemed to be a paternal figure. Nandu followed Seng to his motor vehicle, and they chugged their way to the city centre—Nandu's first car ride. A new and wonderful world was opening up in front of Nandu's eyes. Red was the predominant colour on most houses and temple-like structures, along with touches of gold on the roofs and tilted windows.

During the long ride to the destination, Nandu spotted the stark differences in the income levels in the city. On one hand were the well-dressed men with their sleek hair and leather shoes and on the other were the bare-backed labourers crossing the streets with heavy loads that caused them to stoop.

Very soon, the car stopped in a plush locality. Nandu was told that it was very close to the famous Shanghai Club, located at No. 2, the Bund. Seng pointed to a three-storeyed red-brick building that housed the club, telling Nandu a bit of its history. The British had built it in 1910, and it was frequented by some of the most powerful people in Shanghai. 'Mixing business with pleasure,' Seng told Nandu with a wink.

He added, 'I will make you a member of this building. Then you will be able to see and admire the thirty-four-metre black and white marble bar, the Long Bar. You know, men long to step in there. You are very lucky; everything is arranged for you. Rich and famous Chinese men hobnob with the British and Japanese here. As an honoured guest, you will be seen, but you will hear a lot more. Don't worry, we will train you. I and Ms Lily. Ah! I didn't mention Lily. She is a delicate flower, so polished and beautiful. You will soon see.' He finished this sentence with another wink. Nandu was getting used to the winking and half smile, but he was yet to figure out an appropriate response.

Seng and Nandu entered a three-storeyed building, which looked old but was well-maintained. A mahogany staircase took them to the first floor. Nandu was asked to wait in a huge hall, which was sparse except for a green marble table with an intricate-looking Chinese vase kept on it. Close to the walls were rows of chairs in red velvet upholstery. The hall was probably used to socialize; the vast open space was likely a dance floor. The walls, covered in mahogany panelling, had impressive portraits of the Chinese gentry. Since Nandu didn't have a watch, he wasn't sure how long he waited. He sat down on one of the chairs after some time.

Seng eventually returned with a lady smoking a cigar in a holder behind him. She was dressed in a bright red silk cheongsam, which had delicate embroidery on it. She was breathtaking with her porcelain skin, long red nails and curvaceous body. Her long hair was neatly pinned on top, and she wore tasteful shoes and jewellery.

Seng introduced her. 'Ms Lily is the owner of this house, your landlady and also your coach.'

Lily bent her head slightly, toying with the string of pearls around her delicate swan-like neck. Nandu had never seen anyone so beautiful and elegant, yet so distant. Unsure of how to greet her, he folded his hands in namaste.

Lily chuckled and said, 'Ah, India! I like your culture. It's a pity that your country is in shackles, but we are here to change that, isn't it?'

Nandu didn't know how to react. *Is this a trap to test my loyalty, or does she genuinely mean it?* Seeing him flummoxed, Lily waved a petite hand in the air and said, 'Never mind.

We have plenty of time to discuss this. You must be tired. It is so far from your loved ones, a strange land with strange-looking people. I won't bother you today. You must rest. I will show you your room and send some warm soup and rice. It will nourish your soul and body. Tomorrow, we can start afresh.' She beckoned him to follow. Seng disappeared behind a velvet curtain.

Mesmerized by her, Nandu picked up his small duffle bag and followed Lily up the stairs like an obedient child. His room was on the second floor. It was beautifully decorated with a canopy bed, a dresser, a writing desk and a closet. There was a small washbasin and an ornate mirror, too. She pointed to the washroom, which was adjacent to the room.

Nandu had never stayed in such a plush room or had such a large bed and closet to himself. He was used to sleeping in a cramped position, barely able to stretch his leg, and living out of a suitcase. This opulence was new. He felt like a lord, a high-ranking official, a part of the gentry.

Lily provocatively leaned on the door, her cheongsam parting to reveal shapely legs that were white and smooth. Nandu looked away, wondering why his heart was pounding. Lily probably read his thoughts. 'I must go now. Your food will be served in your room. Tomorrow, I shall invite you for a proper meal. We can talk more then. The closet has clothes stitched as per your size, please feel free to use them. I am sure you will be comfortable. Goodnight!' she said and walked away, her heels clicking on the floor.

Nandu sat on the edge of the bed. He was nervous, but he discarded all thoughts, changed into fresh clothes, washed his face and waited for food. He wanted to go to sleep. Too many things, most of them beyond his comprehension, had happened in the last few days. Sleep and food were needed to calm his racing mind and to take stock of the situation.

The next morning, after a hearty meal, he was summoned to meet Lily. She spoke about the situation in the country—the increase in the number of Japanese troops, the intentions of Prince Asaka, the green zone in Nanjing, the advancing troops.

Sensing his discomfort, Lily placed her hand on his and pressed lightly. 'It is okay, my dear.'

Nandu blushed. This was the first time a woman had addressed him as 'dear'.

'I am here to explain everything to you. You will fit into the gentry in no time, but I am sorry, these ill-fitting clothes must go. Your thick hair needs to be combed with cream. I am presuming you don't drink, but you will need to. You are going to befriend powerful officials in the Japanese army and wealthy Chinese men. We have traitors amongst us. You are going to help us and the British officers. I will teach you, slowly and gradually ... very slowly,' she said and moved closer to him.

Nandu was very uncomfortable. His cheeks were burning, and he was sweating profusely. Lily realized he was on edge and moved back. Throwing her head to a side, she laughed, 'Oh! I have quite a bit of work on my hands. They have sent someone who still smells of the village.'

Nandu's pride was hurt. He retorted, 'I am a good learner. I will brush up on my English and sense of style. I only need a little guidance.'

'Only a little, huh? Only a little,' she repeated and left the room, brushing her legs lightly against his. From the hallway, she called out to him, 'Wait in your room. Mr Seng will take you to your bosses this afternoon. Your white masters will explain the job to you. Mine is already clear!' She again tilted her head and laughed. There was something about her laughter. It was a little charming and a little flirtatious, yet it seemed dark and evil, somewhat sinister. Nandu felt as if he was sinking, unsure of whether he would be able to swim back to the shore.

Seng came later that day and took him to the British headquarters. The building was a maze, and after traversing many staircases and alleys, Nandu stood before his designated officer. *You see one, you have seen them all*, he thought as he saw his boss.

Curled moustache, broad shoulders, gruff voice, coarse red hands, folds on the neck, freckled nose and square jaw—they all looked the same, their language was the same, their instructions were identical. This time, it was Sergeant Timothy, or Tim, who wanted every detail to be reported to him. He began by pointing out how expensive Nandu's posting was but added that his record showed that he had the capability to pull this off. Nandu was told to quickly learn the tricks of the trade from Lily and start mingling in the elite circle to gather information.

Returning to his room, Nandu wondered what lay ahead. He was supposed to meet the British, befriend the Chinese, keep the British and the Germans informed and work against the Japanese by pretending to be their closest ally. *Where is India and all my brothers who are sacrificing their lives in this?* He saw no solution, no way to help the Indian cause. How would he establish contact with the revolutionaries again? He didn't want to lose his identity in a gilded Chinese clubhouse. Holding his head in his hands, he knew that he had no option but to continue down this path until he found a way to reconnect with those fighting to free his motherland.

17

Shanghai was a bustling city with vibrant trade and a robust economy. Nandu started soaking in the culture by walking around. To him, walking was the best way to know a place. It was what he had done in Amritsar, Delhi, Calcutta and Rangoon.

Thanks to his lessons with Lily, his Indian accent was being replaced by a drawl. Lily was a hard taskmaster. Every time Nandu failed in rolling the words, she would make him practice again. Sometimes, she insisted that he keep a hard-boiled sweet in his mouth and then speak.

Nandu was also learning how to use cutlery. He knew which spoon to use for soup and which one to pick up to stir his tea. He stopped using his fingers to eat and could bend his wrist at a certain angle to slice the chicken. Licking his fingers was strictly prohibited. He learnt how to wear a tie, understood which tie went with which shirt, knew how to wrap a silk muffler around his neck and even started rubbing a bit of perfume behind his ears and on his wrists. What surprised him was that perfume differed according to gender. All he had seen was his mother's bottle of attar, that too was brought out only for special occasions. He also became familiar with whisky, gin and tonic, and how to mix drinks or add a dash of lime. He also picked up a few dance steps, something his broad frame and two left feet did not make easy for him.

Outside of his lessons, he walked along the banks of the Yangzi river. He would observe the busy ports, become a spectator in the rallies and meetings organized by labourers on strike, and sometimes visit the French, British or American colonies. The purpose was to learn as much as possible, to hear and pick up information that was worthy of being reported back to his superior, Sergeant Timothy.

As with any prosperous city, Shanghai had its fair share of vices. It wasn't uncommon to hear about mob fights, gangs and killings. However, that was the local police's concern. Nandu was only bothered about the politics and the power game. And he was getting ready to play a part in it.

Nandu's walks soon showed results. He connected with Jivat Singh, who was also from Punjab and had come to China as a trader. Jivat traded in saffron, spices and whatever else he felt was in demand. Nandu was elated to meet someone he could talk to, but he took care to keep up his cover of being a silk merchant.

While discussing the political scenario and freedom struggle in India, Jivat spoke about Mohan Singh from the Punjab Regiment and Mohan's proximity to the Imperial Japanese Army. 'I think our dream of an independent India will come true soon. We hear that there is a chance of war brewing in Europe. This is the time to hit the enemy, when they are weak. There is activity in the Malay Peninsula, and the small Indian community in Shanghai is doing all that it can. We will be glad if you can join us,' Jivat said to Nandu.

Nandu couldn't believe his luck! He wanted nothing more than to serve his country. 'How can I help?' he asked eagerly.

'We need money, arms and ammunition. We will be happy with whatever you can contribute.'

By now, Nandu had supplemented his salary with the silk trade. Letters had been exchanged and Ajit, his childhood friend, was his business partner in India. He decided to use Jivat's trade route and connections to send the choicest silk back to India to be sold at a good profit. Ajit would send Nandu the proceeds of the sale and support Nandu's family financially.

Over the next few months, Nandu, the businessman, began prospering, thanks to the Japanese raw silk exports quadrupling with the decline of China's Qing dynasty. He started exporting raw silk to India and other southeastern countries, which impressed people.

His spy training, too, was almost complete. He could distinguish between forks, he could mix drinks, dress impeccably and match his socks and tie. The British government had spent a lot of money on him and were now waiting for him to gather information from the Japanese intelligentsia.

Soon, Nandu received his membership of the Shanghai Club. He became popular with the British and the Chinese and made inroads into the Japanese inner circle. Most of the men belonged to the Imperial Japanese Army and always spoke in hushed tones. It was evident that they were on a mission. Nandu needed to figure it out quickly.

One name that Nandu heard a lot at the club was that of Huang Jinrong, who was believed to control half of Shanghai. Lily's proximity to the detective-turned-gangster, nicknamed 'Pockmark', was known to everyone. Jinrong ran a gang known as the Green Gang that committed organized crimes. Everybody knew about it but he was never caught let alone convicted. Being a part of the police force gave him an additional advantage over the other petty criminal gangs operating in the city.

Very soon, at a house party, Nandu met him. Jinrong took an instant liking to Nandu and assured him that any information he needed could be obtained from his boys. That evening, sharing space with the rich and famous, Nandu felt that he was finally where he belonged. His life looked picture-perfect. His mornings were spent negotiating with his contacts in Bombay who were eager to buy from him and passing on the information and coordinating with Ajit. His evenings passed in the Shanghai Club, accompanying Lily to parties or attending musical events and film shows.

A magical world lay before him. Information from the Imperial Japanese Army was flowing easily, without renewed effort from Nandu. The British officers, meanwhile, were happy to know the exact location of the Japanese navy, their activities in the Malay Peninsula and their attempts in Singapore.

As the profits poured in, Nandlal started handing over portions to Jivat Singh. He felt his conscience was clear. He felt he was purging himself of his indulgence and sins by contributing to the Indian freedom movement.

Jivat Singh always tried to explain to Nandu how the money had been disbursed, that it was being sent to India or the Far East, where it was spent on ammunition or training youngsters. Each time, Nandu would wave his hand in dismissal. 'Jivat, you are my brother. We are both dedicated to the same cause. Our paths maybe different, but please know that I trust you and know that you will not misuse my hard-earned money. I have faith in you. I wish I could do more, maybe leave all this and be involved directly with the movement. But I believe I lack the courage to face a baton or the gallows. I feel torn between two worlds, which has been the case since I left my village. Sometimes I don't know what is right or wrong. Was I right when I left my mother crying on the doorstep of our house? Look at the expensive clothes I am wearing. I don't know whether the money I send reaches my brothers or not. I don't know what they are doing. I pretend to be their provider, but all I am doing is sinking into indulgence. My brother, the money I put in your hands is the least of my worries. I am glad that I have you in this alien world,' Nandu said without a pause, his eyes moist.

Jivat was a wise man who had faced a similar predicament. He understood Nandu's mental state. He placed a hand on Nandu's shoulder and said, 'I know what you are talking about. When I came here a long time ago, I felt the same way. You are a good son of your mother, of your motherland. What you are doing now, the indulgence you talk of, is something that you need to do. It is your mask, the part you are playing as an actor. My dear brother, one day everything will be all right. We will be back home in an independent country. That day, we will sit together, stare at the yellow mustard fields and drink large glasses of thick buttermilk.'

Nandu started laughing. 'Oh! Please don't remind me of buttermilk. Just the mention of saag and roti makes my mouth water. One day, my dear brother, we will return to our mothers and our motherland.'

The two parted ways a while later, after speaking about all that they had left behind and promising to meet very soon.

That night, Nandu stared at the window that reflected lights from the shops nearby. He didn't remember when he fell asleep, but he woke up to light in his room. The door to his room was open and he could see Lily's silhouette in a slit cheongsam, a shapely leg visible against the light.

In a soft voice, she apologized and explained that she was very disturbed. She then slithered into his bed and hugged him. As she kissed his face and neck, Nandu was lost in thoughts of Vimla's warm body next to him, her gold bangles tinkering and the red shawl his mother had set aside for her daughter-in-law.

Lily's sweet perfume enveloped his senses as he experienced a beautiful sensation. Vimla seemed to be with him, breathing softly into his ears and caressing him. He didn't want to wake up from this dream-like state. He wanted to let this feeling linger. When it came to an end, Vimla's yellow scarf had mixed with the yellow of the mustard flowers and they were running through the fields. Nandu woke up to the fluttering of the curtain and sunlight streaming into the room.

In the morning, as she placed the breakfast tray on his table, Lily smiled and said, 'Your training is complete. You can win over the hearts of women, just as you are doing with the men.'

Nandu blushed and attempted to apologize, but Lily simply held her long finger on her red lips and whispered 'shh' before disappearing into the house. Nandlal knew that he had lost his innocence. He felt ready to conquer the world.

18

There was a sudden air of unrest in the city. Something was going to happen, but nobody knew what or when. Perhaps everyone in Shanghai felt it, or maybe it was just Nandu. He wanted to discuss this with Lily, but she seemed to be avoiding him.

Lily was busier than ever and rarely invited him to accompany her. She disappeared for days and returned exhausted, unwilling to talk about her life. If Nandu asked her anything, she shook her head and said things were changing. Once, she even said, 'Hell is going to break loose. The sky will fall, burning with a putrid smell.'

Nandu did not understand and ultimately gave up. Perhaps her opium consumption was driving her crazy. He told himself that there was nothing he could do about it, that she was not his responsibility, that he needed to focus on what he had to do.

A couple of times, he spotted Huang Jinrong and his boys frequenting the house. It did not look pleasant. Nandu was cautious about not getting involved in the Green Gang's affairs. Jivat had warned him of their ruthlessness.

Jinrong was involved in criminal activities ranging from smuggling and kidnapping to murder. He had a chain of opium dens, which people said were managed by his wife. He was known for human trafficking and was the owner of several brothels in the city. Being in the police, he was beyond anyone's reach. He was excessively cruel and did not spare anyone who crossed him.

In the winter of 1932, Shanghai seemed to have lost its charm. A thick mist hung in the air, and everything looked bleak. The poor huddled by the roadside, burning scraps of paper, pieces of wood and anything else they found to keep themselves from freezing. The black smoke enveloped the city in a sense of hopelessness.

What followed was labour unrest and people starving. Prices of food and other products skyrocketed. Most people were forced to replace turnip and cabbage broth and mutton stew with bone soups. Nandlal's life, encased in a bubble funded by forces beyond the commoner's imagination, went on as usual, unaffected by poverty or hunger. Information was gathered and passed on, and he was paid for doing his job meticulously. Bales of silk were bought and sold and sent abroad, although the increasing price was worrisome. But, overall, there was not much deviation in his life.

Nothing significant happened on that January morning. The New Year celebrations at Lily's household had just ended. Some pieces of decoration still hung on the walls and doorways; fluttering scraps of golden paper and paper lanterns that served as a reminder of the night of merriment with free-flowing wine and delicacies.

Lily seemed to be at ease playing the perfect hostess. After spending one night in each other's arms, she had distanced herself from him. Nandu and she never became intimate after that. It was a subject that was left unspoken as if it was taboo.

Nandu went about his usual business that morning. He worked on the new import duty and negotiated prices. He was slated to go to the club that evening. After calling it a day, he decided to go home for a shower and to change. He expected the night to be long, thanks to the club members' lengthy discussions about the political scenario. A visit to each table meant an overload of information that needed to be sorted, compartmentalized and remembered before it was documented and reported.

It was rumoured that a sect of ultranationalist Japanese Buddhist monks that was shouting anti-Chinese slogans in the city was attacked by a mob. Some of them were injured, and a couple were killed. Civil unrest and boycott of Japanese products followed. Also, there were discussions that over thirty Japanese ships had lined up near Shanghai's shoreline, with over two thousand soldiers ready to attack the Chinese quarters in the city. Nandu was trying to gather as much information as possible. As a result of unrest brewing all over the city, his evenings were turning out to be more tiring than the days.

As Nandu entered the hallway and went up the stairs, he felt something sticky under his shoe. He looked down and gasped. A trail of blood that seemed to lead to his room. He raced up with his heart in his mouth.

What Nandu saw became a recurring nightmare for the rest of his life. Sprawled on his bed, on rumpled sheets and blanket, was the mutilated body of Lily. Her cheongsam was torn, her mouth was parted, her eyes had rolled back as though in fear. A few strands of her beautiful hair lay on the pillow, as if they had been torn out. She had been stabbed several times and her cheeks had been slit with a sharp knife. Her body looked ghoulish.

Nandu tasted the bile rising in his mouth and rushed to the washroom. Holding on to the sink, he splashed water on his face and tried to stop his legs from shaking. He couldn't imagine why anyone would engage in such a barbaric act. He didn't know what to do.

Once his head stopped spinning and his eyes adjusted to the light, Nandu saw that his cupboard had been searched and his clothes were strewn across the floor, some of them lying in the blood that had pooled on the floor. Nandu slumped on the chair next to the bed. Each time he looked at Lily's body, he had to rush to the washroom.

What dark secrets was she harbouring that led to such a fate? A sense of unease engulfed Nandu. Though only a few moments had passed, it felt like an eternity to him. Suddenly, Nandu stiffened. He heard a noise in the hallway. *Have the killers come back for me? Am I their target? What are they looking for? Or is it the police?*

Luckily, it was Seng. He let out a muffled scream on seeing the scene before him. 'Good God! Nandlal, when did this happen? How? Did you see the killers? Who could do this to her?' Seng shot a flurry of questions at Nandu but received no answers except a blank look.

Seng was a wise man. He hauled Nandu up from the chair. 'You must pack your belongings and leave immediately. Do you hear me? Leave immediately. RIGHT NOW! They are coming for you. I know they are, so just go.'

Nandu shook off his stupor. There was nothing much to pack. Most of his clothes were on the floor. From an inner compartment of the cupboard, he withdrew a box with money and some letters, which he packed along with the few clothes that were still in the shelves.

He stood near the door for a while. His head reeled, and he swayed a bit. Seng quickly caught him and said, 'You won't be able to go alone. Wait, I will drive you. Say nothing to anyone, nothing at all. Let me see how I can manage this macabre scene. Wipe your shoes with a cloth and throw them on the road, preferably somewhere far.'

The streets were silent as the two of them tiptoed out of the house. Nandu felt very sorry at leaving Lily's body like that, without arranging a funeral. However, his rational self knew that the funeral would not be immediate. The case would go to the police and there would be an investigation. After that, who knew how long it would take?

Seng wanted to know where he could drop Nandu. 'Do you have anywhere to go? I would, however, advise that you leave the city at once. Now, if possible. If they are after you, they will find you. I will not be able to save you, just like I couldn't save her. I would also suggest that you don't meet any Chinese officials or friends. No one is above the Green Gang. Sooner or later, you will be handed over to them. Do you have any Indian or Japanese friends?'

'Do you think this was done by the Green Gang? Was it Jinrong? What do they want from me?' Nandu asked.

'My dear brother,' said Seng, 'apart from silk, you trade information. And information is valuable. Any person who has information, that too correct, is powerful. Jinrong is the king of this town. I am not sure who did this and why, but I do know that I have lost a dear friend and a good human being. She had her vices, but she was like a lotus flower who kept herself floating above the muck. You may have heard about the Japanese Buddhist monks whose anti-Chinese slogans led to their death and unrest. I don't know what their purpose was, and why the arrival of the monks from a particular sect created so much chaos. Lily was helping them, which is why many considered her a traitor. We Chinese can be very unkind to those who betray us, or even consider betraying us.'

Nandu sat numb, clutching his bag while Seng spoke. His mind was racing, trying to decide the next course of action. The words 'information' and 'traitor' were ringing in his ears. He turned around and said to Seng, 'Take me to Kiyoshi's office. He is my business partner; he will find a way out for me. But, before that, I need to meet my friend Jivat Singh. I must tell him that I am going. Can you take me to him?'

'That might be risky. I suggest you go to Kiyoshi's office and nowhere else.'

'No, I must meet Jivat. I simply must. Please take me there.'

After some convincing, Seng agreed. A breathless Nandu rushed inside and spent a considerable amount of time explaining the situation to his friend. Jivat didn't understand immediately; he knew nothing about Nandu's real assignment in Shanghai.

Finally, hugging Nandu, Jivat said, 'My dear brother, I didn't quite understand what you just told me. Why would members of the Green Gang chase you? You are an ordinary merchant like many of us. I just hope you stay safe. I will send the money to your family in Punjab and write to them that you will be busy for some time, and that it might be a couple of months before you get in touch with them. Promise me that you will let me know when you reach a safe place.'

A tearful Nandu bid goodbye to Jivat with a hug and promised to keep in touch. It was a promise that he honoured.

Seng then took Nandu to Kiyoshi's office. Kiyoshi expressed concern and said that he was aware of the trouble brewing in Shanghai. He was leaving for Kobe in Japan the next morning on the *Heian Maru*, a passenger liner of the Nippon Yusen Kabushiki Kaisha company. 'You can come with me. I can take you to Kobe. There are hundreds of Indians there. You can settle down there, and we can resume our trade. Things are getting dark in Europe, but there is still a demand for our silk. It will sell at even higher prices. What do you think?' Kiyoshi asked.

Nandu immediately agreed. He took leave of Seng, who was happy that Nandu would move to a safe place soon. Nandu settled into a corner of Kiyoshi's office for the night and dozed off in a chair, oblivious to the fact that he had not eaten since the afternoon. His restless mind, haunted by Lily's mangled body, was faced with an uncertain future once again.

KOBE

19

The journey to Japan was uneventful. Most of the time, Nandu sat on his berth on the lower deck, holding on to his bag tightly. It held the result of all his hard work, which he was not prepared to let go. He never liked travelling by sea. It made him feel very sick. His stomach was churning, and he was exhausted from the running around. He didn't have a proper meal for some time and what he wretched out was only bile. He went to the upper berth to discuss his prospects with Kiyoshi and the discussions gave him hope, all was not finished. Though the Shanghai chapter was behind him, he couldn't erase what he had witnessed and kept wondering why Lily was murdered, who killed her, and what they were trying to find in his cupboard. All these questions, for which there seemed to be no answers, did not let him sleep or eat.

Kobe was a bustling city, but it was very different from Shanghai. It was clean, and the morning air had a tinge of chill. The people were polite and neatly dressed. Hyogo Port was designated for foreign trade, which included products like rice, porcelain, pearls, toothbrushes, tea, sake, camphor and peppermint oil. The bustling port area housed several steamship companies and trading offices.

Nandu liked the vibe of this thriving city. While business was on his mind, so were the British officials who were yet to be informed of his sudden departure from Shanghai.

After a restful day in the basement of Kiyoshi's Kobe office, Nandu went out. He buttoned up his jacket and tried to locate a phone booth. The phone call was not very pleasant; his decision to leave was not accepted kindly. He was asked to explain why he had chosen Kobe over Tokyo when the latter had a larger number of Indian revolutionaries. Nandu gave in and agreed to move to Tokyo as soon as the environment was conducive enough. Names and addresses were jotted down, and Nandu was instructed to meet his new reporting officer soon.

Over the next two months, Nandu befriended Anandilal Sharma and Hashmukh Shah, both wealthy Indian merchants who traded in rice, camphor and pearls and imported spices and jute. Since neither of them dealt in silk, they were happy to partner with Nandu and use his expertise to increase their portfolio.

Nandu also got to know Takashi, a young man his age who worked closely with Kiyoshi. Takashi was very eager to learn about India and its culture. He took Nandu around to eat, showed him the city and taught him how to navigate his way around. With him, Nandu experienced simple joys like having tea and his first bite of Japanese tempura.

Nandu, who was still living in Kiyoshi's basement, started house-hunting. This was a first for him. So far, he had stayed in places that were arranged for him by his white masters. Most landlords, given the language and cultural barriers, were not willing to rent to a stranger and foreigner. Both Anandilal and Hashmukh offered him a place in their households, but Nandu wanted to be on his own. He needed time and space to comprehend all that had happened since that night in Shanghai. He craved for a bed beside a window, from where he could gaze at the night sky.

Nandu mentioned his predicament to Takashi, who haltingly suggested that Nandu stay at his cousin's house. 'I would like to apologize. I don't mean to push my case. I mean, that of my cousin, lest you feel that I am using your situation to my advantage, to allow my cousin to earn some money. Please don't think that is the case.'

Nandu assured Takashi that he was not taking advantage of him but being of great help. Takashi described the house to Nandu and mentioned that his cousin was a single woman with an ailing mother. They had been wealthy once but had fallen upon hard times after the demise of his uncle. Renting out one of the rooms would help them earn some money, but they were very cautious given that the house had no male members. Takashi thought that a tenant who was a friend would be a safe bet. It was decided that both of them would visit the house and decide on the rent.

The next morning, Aiko*, a petite and frail woman, opened the door. Something about her reminded Nandu of Vimla. Maybe it was the petite frame, the kind eyes or the long and delicate fingers. Nandu looked around the house and asked Aiko some questions, which she answered in broken English, without looking up from the floor. Nandu decided to move in immediately and handed over the advance rent to her.

The room offered a view of the sky. Nandu fixed his eyes on the moon and thought about his life, which he was trying to bring back on the designated path once again. He was setting up his business again, and accommodation was no longer an issue. All he needed to do now was to establish a link with the British officials.

That part of Nandu's life resumed with a slight reprimand and advice to consult the intelligentsia if a sudden departure had to be made in the future. After that, Nandu's reporting officer in Kobe gave him the usual instructions to file reports every week and provide a phone number where he could be reached in case of an emergency. He was advised to stay alert and be discreet as he was in the enemy's den.

Weary from listening to the same processes, Nandu entered a tea house.

A booming voice hit his ears without warning. 'You need a cover. Without that, you are in danger.'

'Huh?' Nandu looked up.

Standing in front of him was a burly white man in his forties, almost blocking the light. 'May I?' he asked and pointed at an empty chair.

Nandu agreed out of politeness, but he was reluctant to speak to strangers.

'You are an Indian, isn't it? I was in India, in Lucknow Residency. Oh, what a place! Good food, good buildings, good weather and good girls,' he said with a wink.

Nandu, who didn't like the man or his manners, preferred not to answer. He was sure about one thing. The man before him, who introduced himself as Bob and declared his last name to be irrelevant, only needed someone to listen to him. He claimed to be a trader in anything profitable: sandalwood, tea, pearls, spices and other fancy-sounding stuff. He had suffered a loss after investing a large amount of money in elephant tusks which made him move out of India. Drifting from one port to another, he had ended up in Japan.

Still unsure of Bob, Nandu introduced himself as a silk trader but was careful not to divulge any secrets.

Bob started handing out advice to Nandu. 'Don't invest much. There is a lot of unrest in the Malay Peninsula, which is reaching India. Trust me, my news is firsthand. Do you know about karayuki-san? Oh, you don't? You are very naïve, I must say. These are pretty Japanese girls who sail from poor remote villages on their own to other shores to make money. In Singapore, an entire lane is dotted with their houses. There are hundreds of them, and they entertain men like you and me, and the local rich. There, you can get all the information you need. You know, men's tongues become loose when their trousers are down. These girls are my ears and eyes. I pay for them, and they give me all the information I need. I don't want to lose money again; I want to die rich in my own country. Occasionally, I do frequent these places. Yes, I am guilty of that. It has several benefits.' Bob chuckled and shrugged.

The encounter ended soon. Nandu hoped that he would not have to meet this man again. What he did not know was that their paths would cross several times.

Nonetheless, the meeting gave Nandu a sense of direction about how to gather information for his bosses. He had no intention of sailing to the Malay Peninsula or visiting the brothels, but he knew he had to find someone who did. Nandu planned to buy information to sell it. After all, he could not keep chasing trails and betraying the people he pretended to be friends with. He had done that in India, and in Rangoon to an extent, but in Japan, the people valued honour and trust the most. If he was going to make this place his home for some time, he needed to follow the ground rules.

When he thought about 'home', Aiko's image came to his mind. He smiled. He made a note to take some cake with him. The mother and daughter had been very kind to him. They had provided him with all meals and hadn't even mentioned money. Having dealt with the British officers, Nandu felt light and headed towards a pastry shop. *Life has been good. I am blessed*, Nandu thought as he walked home.

20

Life is a mix of rain and sunshine. Some months into his arrival in Kobe, Nandu got bad news from his home—both his parents had died within six months of each other. First, his father had come home with a high fever that proved fatal, and then his mother had taken to bed, pining for her husband and her eldest son. She had passed away peacefully in sleep.

Nandu was devastated at the thought of never seeing them again, and that he had not been there to perform their last rites. His Indian friends in Japan organized a ceremony at one of their houses. It was a sombre gathering.

Aiko understood Nandu's pain. She tried to console him in her broken English. Even her mother invited Nandu to the drawing room and, with Aiko translating, asked about his parents and childhood. A desolate Nandu went back to work after a few days. Walking down to the warehouse, he looked up at the sky and sought his parents' blessings, promising to meet them in heaven one day. He felt guilty; he had not been the ideal son that they expected him to be.

Nandu felt that it was becoming dangerous to be seen gathering information. Somehow, he felt that a pair of eyes were always on him. Be it while walking down an alley, crossing a busy street, enjoying a quiet moment in the tea house, or sitting in the warehouse, he felt a cold stare fixed on him constantly. It was unnerving.

Was it a figment of his fertile imagination, or was it reality? He had no one to confide in; no one knew his real identity. He felt it was best to let everyone think that he was just another trader from India, like the six hundred other Indian traders operating out of Kobe.

Nandu spent every moment thinking of solutions to his predicament. He was finding it immensely difficult to operate as a British spy in hostile territory, and gathering information from a prostitute's den was not something he could bring himself to do. This dilemma, of serving as a double agent, had been bothering him for some time. Alas! There seemed to be no way out. Once a double agent, always a double agent.

Tea rooms proved to be lucky for Nandu. One day, quite by chance, he met another man there. An Indian in his forties, he dressed like a Britisher and spoke like one, too. A frequent visitor at the tea house, he usually sat in one corner with an English newspaper and a cup of tea. He occasionally indulged in a light snack. Whenever Nandu's and his eyes met, he smiled and nodded politely. There was no conversation.

One day, he was standing next to Nandu at the checkout counter. Very bluntly, he asked, 'Will you pay for my tea, too?

Nandu was taken aback, but he said, 'Sure, why not.'

Moments later, as Nandu walked down the narrow alley beside the tea shop, the man caught up with him. He cleared his throat just behind Nandu's shoulder. 'Thank you, sir, for the tea. I could have bought mine; I usually do. Today, I wanted to see whether you would be kind enough to buy me a cup. I was right. You are a kind soul. You must be wondering who this odd human is, isn't it?' he said with a loud chuckle.

Nandu turned around, looked straight into his eyes and said, 'I would be lying if I said no. I have seen you at the tea shop several times. You drink a cup of tea and read a newspaper. Once done, you fold it neatly, tuck it under your arm, pay for the tea and leave. This pattern did get me curious, but I was hesitant to speak to you.'

'You are very observant, I must say. A good quality in your profession,' the man said.

Nandu was surprised, but he didn't show it. 'Thank you. Yes, the silk threads are very fine, and the patterns are woven, so I need to be observant.'

The man waved his hand impatiently. 'Oh, come on. I don't have the time to play these games. I am not interested in your side business, and I am not going to beat around the bush. Let us sit somewhere and talk. I can be helpful in your actual line of work.'

Nandu was very reluctant, but the stranger was persuasive. Soon, they were sitting on a bench in a park, with autumn leaves lying in a pile before them. The waning light of dusk lent a ghostly silhouette to everything around them, giving the setting an eerie feel.

The stranger cleared his throat and started speaking. 'I am Arif Ahmed. I was your predecessor. Surprised? Well, I came here from Rawalpindi exactly eight years ago. I did the same job as you. Only, I was a teacher who taught Hindi to all those who aspired to visit or trade with India. Unlike you, I was not dabbling in the silk trade.'

A small pause later, he continued, 'I am jobless now. I was kicked out. And I take all the blame. I fell in love with a woman who was interested in nothing but money. I spent all my money on her. Soon, I became sick. It is my throat; I started coughing up blood. The doctors don't know what it is, but they know that I don't have much time left. I don't want to go back home and become a burden on my brothers. My memory of them has already faded. I want to go as peacefully as possible. No one is going to miss me much.'

Nandu thought that Arif's voice was choked with emotion, but maybe that was his imagination. Maybe it was his illness that made him sound like that.

Taking slow, deliberate breaths, Arif started speaking again. His words came out as barely a hiss. 'When you are no longer useful to anyone, when you stop serving people, you are finished for the entire world, no one needs you anymore. You are as good as garbage, meant to be thrown out on the streets for dogs. Don't get me wrong. I am not seeking sympathy. I know my time has come, but that doesn't take care of my bills, food and medicines. Oh! No, no, please don't reach into your pocket. I am not begging. I am still a proud man. I want to work, but the army has no place for an ailing man who has made several mistakes. They have no place for a loser like me. But I can still prove to be valuable. Now, I know you are new and trying to settle in. You still need to learn how to navigate your way here. I can help with that. I know where you can get the news and information that the British need; I can get it all for a price. Every time I get you some information, you need to pay me. It can be whatever you can afford. We can meet here at this time every week. If I have something, I will share it. Agreed?'

Nandu contemplated for a while. Arif's story saddened and scared him at the same time. He didn't want to end up like this man—a friendless pauper staring at death. He shared a cigarette with Arif, but that was a mistake. His thin frame shook violently as he was wracked with coughs. As he tried to soothe him, Nandu realized that the cough was not fake. Nandu wanted the information Arif was talking about. He agreed to Arif's arrangement and pressed some money into his palm, after which they parted ways with promises to meet the following Friday.

Arif was a man of many talents. He started furnishing Nandu with information that, as the saying went, was fresh out of the oven. It was invaluable to Nandu's British masters.

There was trouble brewing near the Malay Peninsula, where the Japanese army was gaining ground every day. The British were hungry for details like the number of naval fleets, the name of the commanding officer and whether there were foot soldiers or not. Nandu didn't have answers to all their questions. Sometimes, Arif got him scraps of paper, newspaper cuttings, a secret letter, or a much-thumbed photograph to establish his credibility. With the regular flow of income, which Nandu gave Arif, his health saw gradual improvement. At times, Arif demanded extra cash or gifts. He asked for a new shirt, dinner at an expensive hotel, a jacket to keep warm and even pearls for one of his numerous girlfriends. If Nandu refused, Arif stomped out of the park and returned minutes later to re-negotiate and settle for a less expensive item. By now, Nandu was used to these tantrums. He felt sympathy for Arif, for never being pampered and looked after.

One evening, something unexpected happened. It changed Nandu's life forever. He had decided to retire early after dinner. He woke up with a jolt to someone thumping violently on the door. Still groggy, he managed to open the door. A sobbing Aiko collapsed against him.

From what Nandu could gather, Aiko's mother was gravely ill. Her body felt cold, and her breathing was shallow. Nandu went to her mother's bedroom. His hunch was correct. Her pulse was slow, as was her breathing, and her hands and feet were cold. He instructed Aiko to boil water, give him a couple of towels and heat some oil. Nandu and Aiko started rubbing hot oil on the soles of her mother's feet and on her palms, covering her face and forehead with a hot towel. By the time she started breathing normally, it was morning. Both Nandu and Aiko were tired.

When Aiko came close to Nandu to thank him, he pulled her towards him and said softly, 'You never have to be afraid anymore. I will be there for both of you. You are my family.'

Aiko sighed with relief and nestled against his chest.

Nandu and Aiko got married in a simple ceremony, in the presence of a few friends and family members. They continued to live in the same house, in what was earlier Nandu's room. Nandu was happy to belong to a family again. The simple things gave him joy—the smell of food from the kitchen, which he handpicked at the market, and washed clothes fluttering in the air.

Together, Nandu and Aiko chose curtains and bed linen, tea sets and other decorative items for the house. Nandu was secretly thrilled that his days of living as a vagabond were over.

The young couple soon had a baby boy, whom they named Vijay Raj*. Nandu chose the name 'Vijay', which meant 'victory', hoping that India would soon win its freedom from foreign forces. The baby, a perfect combination of Aiko and Nandu, was as sweet as his mother and as good-looking as his father.

One winter day, both father and son got themselves photographed in an expensive studio. The photo was sent to Punjab. Letters started pouring in from the family, all of whom wished to see the child. Gifts were sent, but unfortunately, by the time they arrived, little Vijay was already too big for them.

Both parents showered their love on the boy. Vijay's grandmother, too, was delighted and started teaching him some syllables so that he could start talking in Japanese. Nandu, meanwhile, taught him to speak Hindi and Punjabi. Vijay surprised everyone by picking up all the languages.

The family itself was doing well, thanks to the flourishing silk trade and the intelligence gathering that was becoming increasingly important in the restless world.

21

The household was getting busier by the day. Little Vijay was naughty and kept everyone on their toes. Aiko was pregnant again. This time, it was a baby girl, whom they named Meera.

Nandu took his role as a father and husband seriously. He spent as much time as possible at home, ensured the kitchen was well-stocked with fresh meat and vegetables, and helped Aiko manage her mother's health.

A young girl from a remote village, who was distantly related to the family, came to stay with them. An orphan, she was happy to be around the children, playing with them and keeping them busy. The family had grown from three to six. Nandu ensured he worked hard to manage the finances well.

Outside the happy home, however, the world was not looking good. After the 1931 Japanese invasion of Manchuria, the relationship with the Chinese had soured. Trade with the Chinese was not doing well. Merchants like Nandu were trying to find other markets. While Thailand was an option, it was still a remote place with a poorly developed transit route. His British bosses, meanwhile, were getting restless for more information.

The Japanese had a secret network of commoners, called the Tortoise Society, across Southeast Asia, mainly in the Malay Peninsula. Anybody could be a potential spy—teachers, doctors, tourists, the Chinese, the Koreans. The trust factor was eroding, and information was reaching the headquarters through various sources, which meant that Nandu's information needed to be up-to-date and authentic.

Nandu had not been able to develop his channels in the way he wanted to; he had been caught up at home and taking undue risks was not an option with two growing children, a wife and other dependents. His only field asset was Arif, who would sometimes vanish for days together. The British officers in Kobe were not happy with Nandu's performance and kept warning him about his negligence.

Nandu was tired of being a British spy and tried to find ways to get rid of the position. His new cohort of businessmen from India were secretly funding the Indian independence movement in the Far East. Nandu joined hands with them and the Indian community in Japan, who were tied to the cause of Indian independence. He was focused on establishing the Indian Independence League, which was slowly gaining ground and becoming a force to reckon with in the Malay Peninsula. With Anandilal and Hashmukh, he approached other Indian business owners to donate generously. Together, they organized collection drives for money, jewellery, precious metals and stones, which were sold to generate funds for the soldiers.

Nandu also shared the information he received from Arif with his friends. Of course, he did not divulge his source.

They were overjoyed to hear that war was brewing in Europe and that the British army was fighting on several fronts. This meant their force was weakening, which would result in loosening their hold over India.

Nandu used his abilities to translate, type and pen speeches for small gatherings. These gatherings were initially organized in houses, with the women rustling up food and snacks, but as they started to grow bigger, party halls were rented under the garb of celebrating Indian festivals. Men met in secrecy and planned entire operations to help the revolutionaries in India and the Far East.

Nandu also provided his friends with information on military developments across the world. They heard that power was on the rise in Germany, which was ready to challenge the British. Indians abroad were excited at the prospect and even thought of establishing links with Germany to get some help in overthrowing the British Raj.

With lots to be done, Nandu wanted to focus his undivided attention on doing more for his country. He still dreamt of returning to a free India, of standing in his mustard fields and breathing the fresh air. Often, at night, he would tell Aiko stories of his village, his parents, his sister and the red silk shawl that his mother had made for her daughter-in-law.

Aiko would always assure Nandu. 'You are the father of my children. Wherever you go, I will follow. I will be happy with you even in your village. I am unfortunate that I never met your parents; I wish I could. I hope they bless us from wherever they are.'

'Yes, they are. They definitely bless us and the kids,' Nandu would reply, feeling a sense of satisfaction as they lovingly looked at their sleeping children and then at each other, drawing closer and savouring the peace.

It was sheer luck that Nandu escaped the Battle of Shanghai, which claimed almost four thousand lives, including those of foreign nationals. He left the city two days before that.

The Sino–Japanese relationship was in turmoil again. One day, Arif came running. He looked exhausted and was breathing heavily. Nandu offered him a cup of tea and asked him to calm down, 'Catch your breath and have some tea. We shall talk after that. Everything can wait, nothing is so urgent!'

'No, no. You don't understand. This is a disaster. Everything will end; this is the beginning of the end. All these killings of the innocent will not go unnoticed by Him. This is so wrong!'

Nandu tried calming Arif down, but he kept ranting about what was happening. He spoke endlessly about a nemesis, payback, evil and the last judgement. Nandu wondered if Arif's illness was making him delirious. He realized that Arif could not be his asset for long. As Arif's handler, he would have to slowly phase him out, give him some money to retire, and start looking for an alternative. He would have to choose wisely. With everyone spying on each other, trust was difficult to establish.

Having drained the last drop from his cup, Arif asked, 'You know Prince Asaka? I am sure you do.'

Nandu politely answered, 'I don't know any prince or anyone from the royal family. I have heard about him though. He came back from Europe after an accident, and they say that the limp general rose to power very fast, commanding a portion of the Japanese army. What about him?'

'Well, he is killing everyone in sight in Nanjing. He was supposed to take temporary control as General Matsui was indisposed. In those few days, he ordered a mass killing. The army has gone berserk. They are not only killing indiscriminately but also raping almost every female, be they old or young, and then murdering them. It is ghastly. I saw a few photographs, and my stomach churned.'

Nandu was tense. 'Should we even be discussing it while sitting in Kobe? I am not sure. I fear for my life. I have a household to look after. And there is nothing we can do about it. We need to safeguard our interests. Your information, however, is valuable. I shall pass it on.'

'You are right, brother, but mark my words. The world has gone crazy, be it here or in the West. I have heard that a brutal person has come to power in Germany. I don't know where all these killings will lead, or who will benefit. Yes, the coal in China and the sugarcane in the Philippines are coming under the Japanese imperial forces, but at what cost? Anyway, I think I get too emotional, which explains where I am in life. I won't take much time and will try to meet soon. Things are changing quickly, and I will hopefully have more to share with you,' Arif said and, taking the money Nandu gave him, vanished as quickly as he had come.

Arif left behind a sense of disquiet. Nandu couldn't put a finger on what was bothering him, but he knew something was not right. He got up from the table, left the money for the two cups of tea and started walking home. His head was throbbing. All he wanted was to hold his kids close.

The Sino–Japanese relationship was deteriorating rapidly. After Nanjing, the next incident to cause turmoil was the Marco Polo Bridge incident in a district outside of Beijing. The Imperial Japanese Army was engaged in battling the Chinese. People were killed indiscriminately in combat or targeted by the secret services. There were Chinese spies all over the country, trying to find out the next move of the Japanese army. Many people involved with the army were being murdered.

Nandu was under immense pressure to bring accurate information, and Arif was not being of much help. His promptness was a thing of the past; no one knew where Arif was. Sometimes, he would go missing for days, emerging only to extract money with scanty or bogus news. He was often seen with Chinese prostitutes, sympathizing with them, looking as dishevelled as a beggar or a drunkard.

Nandu started looking for alternate assets. During this hunt, he met many shady characters, all of whom claimed to know key merchants, traders and generals. Some even claimed to have an inroad into the Japanese royal family and the inner sanctum of the army, but Nandu knew these were fake.

He finally found two bright Chinese boys who had recently graduated. Chen worked in a cycle store, and Kang worked in a factory that processed fish. They were desperate to avenge what was happening in their country. They reminded Nandu of his younger days, when he was trying to find a way to fight for India's independence. These two boys, too, wanted the Japanese army gone from China. They wanted the slaughter to stop.

After all these years, Nandu had become proficient in tapping into people's emotions and using them to his advantage. He remembered how he had started this game of manipulation in Calcutta, with Asit, which seemed to be centuries ago. Chen and Kang were diligent, and unlike Arif, they reported regularly. Given that there was so much happening across the world, there was no dearth of information.

The raw silk business, meanwhile, was picking up. Japan was exporting almost 80 per cent of the world's requirement. Indian traders in Japan were thriving, and so was Nandu. He acquired a warehouse and employed several people. He contemplated asking his younger brother in Punjab, Balraj, to join him, but Dhyanchand was reluctant to send him so far. He wanted extra hands to tend to the mustard fields. Having his brother work with him remained a dream, much to Nandu's disappointment.

Little Vijay Raj, four years old by now, often came to the office and sat on his father's lap. Nandu would stroke his hair and mumble, 'My prince will grow up and take over my business one day.' Then, turning his son's face towards him, he would add, 'Won't you?'

Vijay would grin and say yes to make his father happy. This way, he knew he might get an ice cream on the way home. He was growing up to be a sharp child, intelligent but insensitive towards other kids his age, and sometimes even towards animals.

Aiko raised this concern with Nandu. She told him how Vijay took pleasure in making his sister cry or throwing stones at birds and rabbits. Nandu dismissed it, saying, 'These are hard times. I want my son to be strong. He needs to grow up to be a man capable of looking after his family. Things are not going to get easier. People are killing each other to gain control over forests, streams and even sugarcane that used to grow in the wild. The world is changing. My wife and my son will have to survive and feed the family if something happens to me. Let him be strong and capable.'

These conversations made Aiko nervous. She knew that her husband was involved in businesses beyond raw silk. But rather than discuss it, she kept quiet and prayed for his and the family's well-being. Her mother's failing health was also weighing heavily on her. Aiko knew in her heart that her mother would not make a full recovery.

The National Revolutionary Army of China, also known as the NRA, was making inroads into Japan. The British were getting edgy. They wanted to know more about what the Japanese were up to. Chen volunteered to become an insider and gather information. Nandu was apprehensive about the arrangement, but there was not much that he could do except be ultra cautious.

Nandu realized that he was double-crossing the NRA, the Japanese army, the British and the Indian revolutionaries, all at once. He was entangled and it was becoming difficult to smooth out the creases.

His friend Anandilal was packing up to go back to India and devote himself completely to India's freedom movement. Nandu was not against this idea, but to travel for months with small children sounded like an uphill task. However, he continued to toy with the idea.

On a balmy summer afternoon, Aiko's mother passed away, leaving Aiko heartbroken and depressed. Nandu had to look after the children and his grieving wife. Seeing her wither away, he felt the loss of his own parents keenly. One never really got over the sorrow of losing one's parents, the absence of their caring hand and comforting company.

In 1939, Hitler invaded Poland. The world was divided into the Allied and Axis powers. Japan, engaged in incessant wars, played a key role in the Axis Bloc. Its stronghold in the Malay Peninsula was increasing.

There was pressure on the Japanese to withdraw from China, but that didn't look likely as it would mean an embarrassment. Japan also feared an embargo on certain trade routes and the import of oil. It started looking for reserves of coal, oil and other minerals in the neighbouring countries.

Japan also started strengthening its army on the Hainan Island, which triggered a slowdown of its economy. Resources were being diverted to fund and feed the army, and the price of goods started increasing, making it difficult for an average person to manage expenses.

Nandu often discussed the prospect of going back to India with Aiko. With her mother gone, Aiko had no objections. However, when she asked if she should start wrapping up the household, Nandu's answer was: 'I will tell you when the time is right. But you must prepare to leave your country and travel with me to a country that is yours by marriage.'

A few months after chaos erupted in the world, Nandu's stipend from the British stopped abruptly. When he went to the headquarters, he was told that there had been no inflow of cash, that he would be paid next month.

Nandu managed to give some money to Chen and Kang from his own pocket. Arif had long absconded. The next month was the same, as was the month after it. He was told that the British Army was facing a fund crunch because of war at several fronts—in Europe, in the Middle East and in North Africa. It was building up its fleet to combat the Japanese forces in the Malaya Peninsula. Soldiers were being diverted from across the world to fight in Europe. Nandu learnt that a large contingent of Indian forces was being moved to Poland and other European nations and that some of these soldiers had been abandoned on their way, left behind by their British masters. They were sick or injured, faced a lack of food and were living in deplorable conditions.

Nandu's bad luck had started. His resources dwindled, and the losses kept mounting. Two of his silk consignments never made it beyond the Philippines. Nothing was reaching India, and exporting to Europe was not a possibility anymore. The world was witnessing a disaster. There was no money. The number of people dying ran into many thousands. Beautiful cities were bombed and all that remained was rubble.

Aiko was pregnant again. One evening, when Nandu and Aiko were planning for the days ahead, there was violent knocking on the door downstairs. Both of them stiffened. Meera woke up crying. Nandu asked Aiko to remain in the bedroom with the children.

To his surprise, he saw a young woman, barely in her twenties, standing at the door. She was shivering in the cold. It looked like she had come running. Her breathing was heavy, her cheeks were flushed and her make-up was smudged. It was evident that she was from the wrong side of the town. Her bright make-up and garish clothes were proof.

Nandu ushered her inside and called Aiko. They offered her a glass of hot milk, but she refused it saying that she didn't have the time and had come to deliver important news. Arif had been dragged away by the Japanese army that evening. They had kicked him into a van. Arif had managed to tell her to contact Nandlal and added that he might not be able to hold on for long, that he would surely succumb to torture. The woman left immediately after conveying the information.

Nandlal knew it was time. Arif would not be able to bear the brutal interrogation techniques of the Japanese for long.

He would spill the beans and blurt out that Nandu was the actual informer for the British, that he only gathered intelligence to supplement Nandu's network. The Japanese would not be kind to Nandu and his family. Staying in their country, spying on them and reporting it to the British would mean severe measures.

Nandu understood the gravity of the situation. He knew he had very little time before his and his family's life came under threat. He told Aiko to pack whatever she could in two suitcases and dress the kids in warm clothes. He contacted Hashmukh and decided to take cover in his house.

In the middle of the night, a pregnant Aiko and two sleepy kids were bundled into the car. Nandu left his house for the last time. The house help would stay with Hashmukh for sometime and eventually go back to her village. As he reversed the car, he knew that he was heading towards a life of uncertainty once again. Only, this time he was not alone. He would risk his own life, if needed, to save his wife and children.

22

Nandu and his family hid in Hashmukh's residence for three days and two nights. It was a nightmare. The children didn't understand why they were confined to a small space, why they were not allowed to run around. Aiko, too, was uncomfortable in a makeshift bed. Nandu felt guilty for putting Hashmukh's household in danger, especially because his friend was doing everything possible to ensure Nandu's family was comfortable.

The situation wasn't stable. A servant boy, who was sent to fetch some things from Nandu's house, informed them upon his return that some shady people were lurking around.

Nandu wondered what had happened to Arif, or how much he had divulged to the Japanese. His days and nights were tortured, spent in the fear that they might be caught at any moment. He knew that hiding in a friend's house wasn't the solution. He discussed it with Aiko, who seemed to have resigned herself to fate. She was too tired to argue. They agreed to ask his friends to sell the house and business and send the money to them in India.

Nandu discussed his plans with the friends who came to meet him. They were all unsure as to why he was hiding. After all, to them, he was an ordinary trader. They had no idea that he was a British spy. All Nandu could tell them was that he had come under the Japanese army's scrutiny, that he seemed to have displeased them somehow, which was why they were hunting him down. His friends didn't probe much. They knew that it was a turbulent time.

Finally, it was decided that Nandu and his family would be smuggled to the port, where they would board the *Asama Mura*, which was scheduled to leave the next day, and head to Johor Bahru, a city in the Malay Peninsula.

It was difficult to get a berth on the ship as many people were leaving due to the war in Europe. Japanese fleets were gaining ground in the Malay Peninsula and had already established bases in Songkhla and Pattani in Siam (modern-day Thailand), as the US, the UK and other European nations had imposed an embargo on oil imports from Japan. Major Fujiwara of the Japanese army had the entire place covered with intelligence agencies (or kikans) that were linked with the Malay and Indian pro-independence organizations. Churchill and Roosevelt had already declared that their priority was the war in Europe, and not Southeast Asia. In such a situation, many expats and others hailing from Southeast Asia were rushing back to their countries.

The large sum of money that Nandu offered to the officials had the desired result. Four tickets were purchased for his family till Johor Bahru. Jivat Singh, Nandu's friend from Shanghai, was in Johor Bahru with his family. He was happy to host Nandu and his family.

The next morning, after feeding the children and covering them in enough warm clothes, the family left for the port quietly. The journey was uneventful. Everyone in the small, crammed car was silent. Nandu was only worried about getting caught. There was not much time to lament the loss of money, property and prestige, nor was there any time to bid farewell to all those who had accepted him with open arms when he had arrived in Kobe almost nine years ago.

It was here that he had got married, had his children, built a home and business and led a comfortable life. A twinge of guilt and sadness overwhelmed him. Aiko understood that and placed her hand on his. No words were spoken but Nandu knew that his wife's kind eyes were telling him that it was okay, that they were still together and able to look forward to a new life. He was thankful to the Almighty for his mercy.

The port was crowded with people scuttling to get on to the ship. Everyone was pushing and jostling, trying to be the first one in the line. After a hurried goodbye and promises to meet in free India, Nandu parted ways with his friends who had been his greatest support in Kobe. He wanted to wait a while, but the crowd didn't allow him to do so. He was swept off his feet, trying hard to hold on to his children and wife. It was difficult to maintain balance against the surging tide of people. Determined to leave Japan, Nandu shielded his family with his large frame, clutching onto them and the suitcases as if his life depended on it.

Meera was crying incessantly, and an exhausted Aiko was trying everything to keep her calm. Finally, they found their two berths on the lower deck; the children had to huddle with the parents as there was a shortage of space. It was ill-lit and claustrophobic, with a musty smell. Nandu was worried about his family's health as the journey was long. To top it all, he still didn't have an easy time on ships. Yet, he was glad that they were safe and together. As the ship left the shore, Nandu was flooded with memories: the road that he took every day, their comfortable house, the bakery from where he picked up fresh mochi buns, the smell of deep-fried tempura, the jokes, the festivals that he celebrated with his friends, Arif with his dishevelled look, and the hardworking Chen and Kang. He knew that there was no turning back. He could never go back to Rangoon either, but his parting with Japan was more painful. His eyes became moist, but he quickly wiped them before his wife and children could see.

Through the journey, Aiko felt sick and struggled to eat. The children, too, complained about the sticky rice and potato they got on board. Nandu, meanwhile, made friends with some people heading towards the same destination.

Everyone was worried about escaping the Kra Isthmus unharmed. The Japanese fleet had lined up there, waiting to attack the Malay Peninsula. Everyone prayed that the ship would pass before any military action was taken. God heard their prayers, and the ship passed the canal safely. Many people went to the upper deck to see the line-up of the Japanese fleet, with the flags fluttering in the air. It was a frightening sight.

Most of their time was spent in analysing the implications of the war in Europe and the Far East on India's independence movement. Nandu was glad to hear about the growing Indian Independence League in the region.

When the journey came to an end, tired people with cramps in their legs and suitcases in their hands alighted. They were relieved to feel the ground under their feet after a long time and sent up prayers to their respective gods. Nandu was glad that Jivat had come. As the two friends hugged and cried, the children were amused to see their father crying like a baby.

Jivat was still struggling to establish himself in this small town, which had nothing much to offer. He had opened a grocery shop to keep himself and his family afloat. The small house and meagre income, however, didn't stop him from managing an extra plate of rice and a bed for his friend.

Nandu and Jivat spent a lot of time immersed in nostalgia, but the time was not conducive to taking a pause. Japanese forces had taken over Alor Setar, Sungai Petani and Butterworth in the Malay region and were advancing towards Singapore. Although there were no military attacks where Nandu was, the price of goods was skyrocketing, and people from different parts of the world were coming in in large numbers, fleeing from the war. Nandu and Jivat started doing all kinds of odd jobs: selling goods, working as middlemen, helping fishermen sell their catch, anything that would help them bring food to the table.

Aiko, meanwhile, gave birth to another girl, whom they named Indu*. Nandu managed to rent a small house for them, which had barely two rooms. They moved in at the beginning of December, three months after they came to Johor Bahru. It was very close to Jivat's house, allowing both friends to be together.

In December 1941, news came in of the bombing of Pearl Harbour and the subsequent occupation of Singapore. Nandu heard it all dispassionately. He had nothing to do with these incidents. In fact, at times he felt as if he had staked his life for nothing. When the time came, there was nobody beside him; he had been abandoned. Everything seemed pointless. He wondered if he had done the right thing by leaving his village, the comfort of his house and the love and care of his parents. There was no answer. There was no one to tell him whether the path he had chosen was correct or not.

Often, Aiko would catch him staring at the wall; sometimes he would hold food in his hand but forget to eat. Aiko was scared to see this new side of her husband. He rarely smiled, never dressed up and didn't try to explain politics or what was happening in the world to anyone. Even if she tried to initiate a conversation, he just avoided it or moved away citing some work that needed his attention. Nandu's only solace was playing with his children, holding them close and humming to them. Throughout the day, Jivat and he tried to search for extra work and money. They had only one goal: to provide enough food and necessities for their families. The savings they had were exhausted in dealing with illness, childbirth and getting and maintaining a house.

Jivat was still involved with the freedom movement in India. In 1943, he went to Singapore to attend Subhas Chandra Bose's conference. Bose had come to Singapore to strengthen the Indian National Army and the women's regiment, which was called the Rani of Jhansi regiment, led by Captain Lakshmi Sehgal who was stationed in Malay. Bose declared the existence of Free India, or Azad Hind, and announced the formation of an Indian government in exile, which started functioning from Singapore. The provincial government was recognized by Germany, Japan and a few other countries. The Indians were overjoyed at the thought that Bose would get help from Germany.

Jivat tried to coax Nandu to accompany him to such groundbreaking events. However, Nandu was reluctant. He still feared being identified as a spy who had betrayed the Japanese. Ultimately, Jivat went on his own. This time neither Jivat nor Nandu were able to fund the movement or even raise funds in their poor neighbourhood in Johor Bahru.

There were highs and lows as the world war drew to an end. News of the impending freedom of India, along with the Partition, started coming in. Nandu was worried. He kept urging Aiko that if starvation and death were ordained for him, he would rather be in his own country. Money was kept aside to sail back to India. Soon after India's independence, Nandu sailed home with his children and wife. Jivat didn't want to come, not until the new India had settled down. He wanted to try his luck in Johor Bahru, maybe go to India after building something of his own. Parting with him once again was difficult.

Before leaving, Nandu said to him, 'Wherever I am, there will always be room for you and your family. Come home soon, my dear brother.'

The journey to Punjab was tedious, and Nandu was not very sure of what waited for them at home. He planned to be in Calcutta for a while, where the children would have access to proper schooling, something that would be impossible in his village.

Leaving the Far East made Nandu nostalgic. He thought of the time when he had first sailed to Rangoon. He had been so sick, and Ramcharan had looked after him. Who knew where Ramcharan was. Had he returned to India, or was he still in Rangoon? As Nandu headed towards the ship that was to take them back to India, he was overwhelmed. He had set out as a young struggler, a bit aimless, and tried to find a purpose in life. He was returning twenty years later with his wife and kids, having seen life, with grey strands in his sideburns and fine lines around his eyes. His gait was slower, he spoke slowly and sometimes drifted into silence. Some of the people he had left behind in Punjab were not there anymore. He was apprehensive that he would have to start all over again as a stranger. *Will people remember me? Will they greet me again?* Nandu let out a sigh.

In Calcutta, Nandu managed to rent a small apartment in the heart of the city. It was basically in the attic of a building close to Hogg Market, where Nandu had stayed years ago. The memory of Asit, Beniapara Lane, the alleys and Vimla came flooding back.

It was 1948, and food was scarce. Finding a job was even harder. Refugees had flooded the city. The streets were not safe; looting and killings were common. Nandu tried to put up a makeshift stall to sell clothes. After all, fabric was his first love. Buyers were few, and everyone wanted to buy on loan.

Aiko was worried about her husband. He was not his usual self. Of course, he was doing all that was required of him, but he rarely spoke. Some days, he would just sit and watch the children play or silently have his dinner. When asked about the food, he would murmur to say it was okay. Aiko thought the war was to blame. Leaving behind a life of luxury, his home and his friends had probably pushed him into silence. Who knew what kind of life he had before marrying her, what all he had seen and done?

After struggling for over two years in Calcutta, Nandu decided to go back to Punjab. He wanted to go back to his roots. This decision was welcomed by Aiko. Perhaps the open fields and the backbreaking work of a farmer would be good for his health and mind. The children, who were studying in missionary schools in the vicinity, groaned at the prospect of going to a village. Ultimately, it was decided that the children would stay with their mother in Calcutta. Nandu would come back twice a year with the proceeds of the harvest. Vijay Raj, a responsible teenager, would look after his mother and younger siblings.

For the next thirty years, twice every year, Nandu took a train from Firozpur to Howrah and then a bus to reach his home in Calcutta. When his firstborn got married and had a baby boy, he stayed back to be with his grandchild. The baby became his obsession. He bought a pram for him, played with him and celebrated his birthday with a theme cake and khoi bags.

The spy, the silk trader and the farmer had blended to come together as a grandfather. Nandu's world was his grandson. He used to sit for hours and narrate to him tales of his colourful past. The child understood only some of it, but he waited patiently for his grandfather to finish the story and give him a one-rupee note that would fetch him ice-cream lollies or roasted corn cobs.

At the age of eighty-three, Nandlal's extraordinary life came to an end with an ordinary death. The life that could have been lost in a faraway land was laid to rest amidst family and friends. Everyone had only one thing to say: 'It was a life well lived.'

One chilly winter afternoon in Firozpur, Nandlal Kumar had taken a vow. It was a promise to himself to keep the life he had led a secret. No matter how much his wife or children wanted to know, he would not talk. He finally broke his vow and his silence with his grandson, who understood him at times and tried his best to remember all that he could and preserve some of his photographs.

With his death, the Silk Route Spy's life was lost. No one remembered his contributions to the freedom movement. There was no plaque, no shawl, no certificate for him. The spy had vanished quietly, just like he had lived, a handsome man who blended into any part of the world he chose to be in.

Years passed, and his grandson too left this world very early in his life, perhaps once again to sit beside his grandfather and listen to his tales. Being the sole survivor of his eldest son's family and the wife of his only grandson, I felt the need to tell his story, as if he spoke to me and urged me to write. I hope I have been able to do justice to such an illustrious life.

ACKNOWLEDGEMENTS

Nothing is completed alone. Everything one creates reflects the kindness of others. I am grateful to my late husband, Vijay Kapur, for narrating the story of his grandfather to me and sharing photos from the family album. My sister, Nilakshi Sengupta, continues to encourage me to write. My parents, Mira and Naresh Ranjan Sengupta, and my parents-in-law, Lekhraj and Dorothy Kapur, might be in another realm; yet they are with me.

I would like to thank Suhail Mathur, my literary agent at The Book Bakers, for his constant support, and Bushra Ahmed, my commissioning editor at HarperCollins India, for her valuable inputs and suggestions. I am indebted to you all. Thank you for being a part of the book and for being in my life.

ABOUT THE AUTHOR

Dr Enakshi Sengupta is a prolific researcher and academician. She has twenty-five years' experience working in both the corporate world and in academia. She has a PhD from University of Nottingham and has completed her MBA with merit from the same university.

HarperCollins *Publishers* India

At HarperCollins India, we believe in telling the best stories and finding the widest readership for our books in every format possible. We started publishing in 1992; a great deal has changed since then, but what has remained constant is the passion with which our authors write their books, the love with which readers receive them, and the sheer joy and excitement that we as publishers feel in being a part of the publishing process.

Over the years, we've had the pleasure of publishing some of the finest writing from the subcontinent and around the world, including several award-winning titles and some of the biggest bestsellers in India's publishing history. But nothing has meant more to us than the fact that millions of people have read the books we published, and that somewhere, a book of ours might have made a difference.

As we look to the future, we go back to that one word— a word which has been a driving force for us all these years.

Read.